Exit Page Ten

Mrs Capper's Casebook #4

David W Robinson

Prologue

Good afternoon and welcome to Christine Capper's Comings & Goings, your weekly look at what's been happening in and around Haxford, sponsored today by Terry's Tea Bar. If you want the best, forget the rest and join Terry and his crew in Haxford Market Hall where you're guaranteed good food, service with a smile, and prices that won't tempt you to run a mile.

May was one of the worst months of my life, and I was glad to see the calendar change, heralding what would be the start of a glorious, hot and sunny June. Dennis was still unable to walk or speak properly and needed constant care and attention. My son and daughter-in-law and my next door neighbour helped when time permitted, but most of the time, it was down to me.

And his physical needs were not the only problem. His income protection insurance amounted to only half his usual earnings, a huge gap in our income which, coming on the back of the outrageous rise in energy prices, increases in council tax, and national insurance, and the cost of his prescriptions, we could ill afford. I needed to increase my efforts as a private investigator, get proactive, get out there and seek clients instead of waiting for them to come to me. But how was I supposed to do that when Dennis needed me at home?

Five weeks ago, we had a rosy future, now I was staring into a black hole of despair. And then, as is the wont of fate, I had a phone call from a friendly voice, but one who brought me an unfamiliar tale.

Let me take you back to those first days of flaming June.

Chapter One

You get those days when you just feel like doing nothing. Not really an option with Dennis being the way he was, but even so, that June morning was such a day.

All Cappy the Cat and I knew was a glorious, cloudless sky, the sun beaming down into the back garden, the temperature climbing until, still early in the day, it was just too hot to sit in the conservatory, at which point we dragged the sun lounger out, set it on the lawn and settled down for a lazy morning. By we, I mean me. Even if Cappy the Cat were able to drag the sun lounger out to the lawn, he wouldn't. He was far too lazy.

Wearing a loose, pale blue, sleeveless top and a pair of itsy-bitsy, tweeny-weeny, yellow, non-polka-dot shorts which were too small five years ago and which bared far more thigh than I would dare to show if I were anywhere but my own back garden, I sprawled on the lounger, a pair of fake Ray Bans (I gave eight euros for them in Puerto del Carmen, Lanzarote) shading my eyes, a glass of iced lemonade to hand, and prepared to drift. Cappy the Cat leapt up there without bothering to ask permission, and settled down on my tummy, and that was okay until he tried to sprawl and accidentally dug his claws into the shirt and my bare skin beneath, so I threw him off. He gave me a look of thunder then flaked on the grass alongside the lounger.

This, I told myself, was what life was all about.

Except that it wasn't and it hadn't been since that terrible evening five weeks back, when Dennis was attacked in his workshop. It was now known within the family as The Incident (initial letters capitalised).

His injuries were so bad that I should have been grateful I still had him, but at those times when the pressure was on, when I was at my lowest, the insidious thought that both he and I would be better off if he had died, would sometimes worm its way into my shattered mind.

When it did, I crushed it under a welter of self-recrimination. We had been together for thirty years, and no matter what the ups and downs life threw at us, I could not have wished for a better life partner. He might be mechanically obsessed to the nth degree (if he knew he'd been in an ambulance he would want to know the make, model, and engine size of the vehicle) but he had always been there, a stalwart companion, a good provider, a reliable husband and father to our two children. He tolerated my moods, good and bad, only resorting to his familiar, blunt speaking on those occasions when he believed I was going too far. He put up with the vicissitudes of my various callings – vlogger, blogger, private investigator, radio agony aunt – and what they meant in terms of disruption to our routine, and like any good Yorkshireman, he moaned and groaned his way through life, but it was placid, superficial moaning and groaning, the grumblings of a man contented with life and wife.

And when necessary, he was not slow to defend me. Tall, in good health – before The Incident – he would never stand by and let anyone talk down to me or insult me, and he certainly would not allow them to threaten or intimidate me. During The Incident he had lashed back and injured one of his attackers, but had the assault been aimed at me, he would not have hesitated to step in and fight on my behalf.

How dare I entertain the villainous idea that we would be better off if he was dead?

On that beautiful June morning, it would never enter my head. Dennis was sleeping (the last time I checked) and neither I nor Cappy the Cat knew that it would be the start of a week-long heatwave. In his condition, Dennis didn't have a clue about anything really, although, once he woke up, I would get him out into the sunshine. It would be good for him.

It didn't take long for the heat to get to me. I felt my eyelids drooping, and the soft, summery sounds melded into a hypnotic, soporific drone. Before long, reality began to recede and dreams began to take its place.

With nothing on TV the previous night, I sat through *Pirates of the Caribbean*, and now, as I drifted off to sleep, I found myself transported from the back lawn to a baking hot, tropical island where Deppy and Bloomy were threatening all-out war for the privilege of escorting me from the beach into the jungle, while Once Nightly stood by, hands on hips, feet tapping irritably on the sand, her envious eyes asking what I had that she hadn't which would make me the object of Deppy and Bloomy's desire.

My heroes held me by the hands, tugging me one way and the other, Deppy insisting I should go with him on a slow boat to Scarborough, Bloomy insisting he should show me the bridleway to Bridlington. And Bloomy won, but only because my daughter lived in Scarborough, and the beach at Bridlington was larger and stretched further than that at Scarborough.

And then I was tripping away with Bloomy towards a clandestine clinch in some discreet boarding house where we could be at one with nature, or at least connected as one with nature. So Bloomy was ten years younger than me. What of it? You don't stop to count when the heartbeat and anticipation are on the up.

All good dreams must come to an end, and I never did get to the backstreet B&B because with typical contrariness, my mobile rang. When the phone warbled Blondie's Heart of Glass, the desert island housing Bridlington disappeared, the back lawn re-materialised, and Cappy the Cat looked up, his face a mask of unmitigated disapproval, as if asking, 'why don't you shut that thing off and let me get some sleep'?

I felt the same way. I was the only worthwhile private investigator in Haxford (come to think of it, I was the *only* private investigator in Haxford) and even in the days before The Incident, I had to leave the smartphone switched on in case a potential client rang. True it didn't happen often. Three or four times a year if I was on a good run, which explained why I couldn't afford to risk missing any calls. With Dennis incapacitated, Lester Grimes, one of the partners at Haxford Fixers, had rigged up an alert system which would call my mobile when Dennis pressed the button at his bedside or hit the app icon on his mobile. When it woke me up, I was on instant alert. He had either woken up or was in need of other urgent attention.

But this wasn't Dennis's alarm. It was a call from Haxford Fixers.

With Dennis out of the game, his partners, Lester and Tony Wharrier had taken on a mechanic, Greg Vetch, a man Tony and Dennis knew from their days at Addison's, and Tony had assumed the role of senior partner. I could not begin to guess why they would be bothering me on a sunny, Wednesday morning, so I didn't try. Instead I made the connection.

"Hey up, Chrissy, how's it going, lass?"

It was Lester, the most laid back of the three, and the one with an insouciant attitude to work and life, which for him meant singing on karaoke and an excess intake of Haxford Brewery Best Bitter.

"Lester, do you know what I was about to do with Bloomy?"

"Plant a coupla rose bushes? D'yer gerrit? Eh? Bloomy? Rose bushes?"

"Yes very funny. Can we get you on Britain's Got Talent as the unfunniest comic in the country? Now what do you want?"

"Snot me as wants you. It's Geronimo. He wants a word."

"Well, why didn't he ring me?"

"He didn't like, what with Dennis living in never-never land. You know what he's like, our Geronimo. So backward in coming forward, he meets himself going the other way. And what was you doing with this Bloomy sort? I've told you, when you're getting desperate for a man, I'm first in line."

With anyone else, I might have taken offence at the suggestion, but I'd known Lester for so many years that I was able to ignore it. "Just put Tony on, Lester."

It was a major puzzle. Geronimo was Haxford Fixers' pet name for Tony Wharrier, and if it came to sitting in the Mastermind chair, Tony's specialist subject would have to be repairing the bodywork on cars. In all the years I'd known him, I'd never heard him talk about anything else. I'm exaggerating. TBH, that was more like Dennis (engines in his case) than Tony. Mr Wharrier did talk about other things such as spray-painting cars after the damage was repaired.

I was being unkind. Dennis was obsessed with engines, Tony with bodywork, but he wasn't quite as single-minded as my husband. He was simply boring. I knew he had a couple of hobbies – collecting stamps and vintage postcards – both as tedious as the man himself, but like us, he had been married for the better part of thirty years to a woman who was better educated than him. They had a couple of sons, the mortgage was almost paid off, and Tony (Val too, for all I knew) were drifting into that steady decline towards the pension and long-term indolence.

"Good morning, Christine." He was also more polite than my down-to-earth old man or their other partner. The only time Dennis used my full name was when he was annoyed with me. The rest of the time I was Chrissy or 'hey up, lass'. Naturally, that was in the days before The Incident; days when he could speak properly.

"Good morning, Tony. You wanted a word?"

"Well, not me, but my wife, Valerie."

"Oh."

This was an even bigger puzzle. Val Wharrier was on my Christmas card list, but only by virtue of being married to Tony and only then because he was a partner in Haxford Fixers. Val and I had met many times over the years but our orbits rarely coincided. She was some kind of reader/commentator on books and whenever we got into conversation, she would waffle on about Jack Kerouac and Damon Galgut and Bernardine Evaristo, all of whom I had heard of, but none of whom figured high on my annual shopping list.

"Hello? Christine? Are you still there?"

I realised that many seconds had passed since I last said anything, and even then, it was nothing coherent. "Yes. I'm sorry, Tony. I was drifting. You said Valerie wants to speak to me? Why?"

"I don't know. She wouldn't tell me. Wouldn't even give me a hint. With Dennis the way he is, she doesn't really like to trouble you, but she did ask me to ask you to ring her. Can I give you her mobile number?"

One of the problems with lazing around the back

garden was that I never took pen and paper with me. Why would I need them... short of people ringing me, that is? All right, so I should have them, but I didn't. "Bit difficult, Tony. I've no pen and nothing to write on... other than Cappy the Cat, and I think he might take umbrage at lipstick scrawled all over his back. Could you text me her number and I'll ring her straight away?"

"Yes, of course."

"And you've no idea what she wants?"

"Sorry, no. But she sounded quite, er, not worried, but concerned."

He asked about Dennis, I gave him a brief report, and we ended the call there, and in the ensuing silence, broken only by the sounds of encroaching summer all around us, while Cappy the Cat went back to sleep – how do animals do that? They nod off in a matter of seconds, whereas it takes me ages – I wondered what Val could possibly want.

Word was spreading about Christine Capper. I was well-known as a vlogger and blogger, and since a few days after The Incident, when Radio Haxford appointed me, I was the local radio agony aunt, which in turn had raised my profile as a private investigator, but I could not imagine Val Wharrier being in need of any of those services.

My weekly vlog Christine Capper's Comings & Goings, was popular in and around Haxford, and many people knew me because of it, so it was entirely possibly that she wanted me to do a piece on her and her work. If all she did was read books, it didn't sound like the pinnacle of excitement, and I might have some trouble generating interest. But I couldn't think of any earthly reason why she would need me as a private investigator or an agony aunt.

Thanks to the vlog, many people knew I was a private investigator but I wasn't entirely certain whether Val did. Correction, she did know but I wasn't sure she knew I was a professional private eye and the same might be said of my vlog viewers. There were a number of reasons for this, not least of which was the size of the town. Haxford had a population of about 25,000 and the need for private investigators was small. Over and above that, I was choosy about the kind of work I took on. I didn't do crime. That was the exclusive province of the police, and even though I used to be Capper the Copper, I steered clear of criminal investigations. Having said that, I did help the police pin down Haxford's serial killer, the Graveyard Poisoner, but even that case started out as a simple theft inquiry. And, of course, I was instrumental in solving that business at Haxford Wool Fair in the spring, and I pinpointed the killer in the blackmail case during which Dennis had suffered his terrible injuries.

Other than that, I kept away from criminal matters, and unlike many private eyes, I kept away from bad debts, although I was prepared to trace the debtor and pass the information on to the creditor. People tracing and divorce evidence were my mainstays. Even so, my profile was rising, and the message that I was a professional PI was beginning to permeate Haxford's collective consciousness.

And as for the agony aunt slot... well, if Val needed any of the bland advice I gave out during my weekly, fifteen-minute spot, all she had to do was ring the radio station and disguise her voice. Dennis did it once (before The Incident, obviously) but I twigged him right away.

And as I thought of it, coming up with idea after idea and dismissing them, the reason for Val's call occurred to me. Tony was being unfaithful and she wanted the evidence. She needed me not as a vlogger or blogger, but a private eye.

Tony Wharrier? Unfaithful? So ridiculous I almost laughed at the mere idea. He was a potential gold medallist in the Mr Universal Boring competition, but the thought gave rise to this absurd image of him and a sprightly octogenarian getting all hot and bothered at the sight of a Penny Black or a picture postcard of Southport from 1907, she throwing off her corsets and ripping the string vest from Tony's back.

Tony Wharrier was a more unlikely candidate for adultery than Dennis, and the only way my old man would ever betray me was to buy a Ford Anglia, the one with the cutaway rear window, without consulting me first.

No. If Val wanted me as a private eye, it was not because Tony was unfaithful. So was it her being unfaithful then? It might be justifiable given tedious Tony's general lack of get up and go (although I had never yet come up with any form of justification for adultery) but why would she need me? Perhaps she was going to warn me off. "Listen, you, I have a lover. If Tony tries to hire you, tell him you're too busy." Or maybe her lover was being unfaithful to her and she wanted to expose him as a total love rat, cheating not only on his wife but also his bit on the side.

I was quite at home with this kind of speculation while waiting for a potential client to ring or making my way to a meeting. It helped prepare me for whatever he/she might have in mind. When they first got in touch, people were usually reluctant to talk on the phone. They preferred face to face, and to be honest, so did I.

My smartphone beeped to tell me the text message had come through. It woke Cappy the Cat, who scowled, got up, marched across the lawn and jumped over the fence and into the Timmins's garden where he would no doubt leave a couple of messages expressing his dissatisfaction with life in general, nap time on our lawn in particular.

I made the call and waited to be connected.

"Wharrier Editorial Services, Valerie speaking."

Very formal, business-like. "Val? It's Christine Capper. I had a call from Tony asking me to ring you."

"Oh, hi, Chrissy. Yes, I, er... Look it's difficult to explain on the phone. Any chance you could come and see me?"

"Impossible, I'm afraid. Dennis, you see. He still needs twenty-four-seven care. It's not that I can't do it, but I have to make arrangements first."

"Ah, I thought that might be the case. Well, look, could I come to you?"

Exactly as I anticipated. The answer would preferably be 'no' but the company would be welcome. "As a vlogger?" I asked.

"No. As a private eye."

At this point, I felt it incumbent to stress my

professionalism. In other words, I didn't do this for the fun of it. "I need you to understand in advance, Val, that I don't work for nothing. I have a scale of charges which are not negotiable... well, they're not normally negotiable, but I suppose I could come to some arrangement and call it mates' rates."

"I'm quite all right with your regular charges, Chrissy. Tony did explain that you're licensed and you treat it as a job, not a hobby."

And Tony had it right. There was no requirement in UK law for a private investigator to be licensed, but as an ex police-officer, I felt it necessary when I first opted for the job.

"All right. Glad we've sorted that out. Could you give me some idea of the problem?"

"Murder, Chrissy. The problem is murder."

Chapter Two

The very word brought me up short. "Whoa. Let me stop you right there, Val. If you suspect a murder, you must go to the police."

She was pleading and I had an image of her near to tears. "It's more complicated than that, Chrissy. I am not accused of anything, but the woman the police have taken in is accusing me of accusing her, and I'm innocent. I haven't done anything, but if I don't sort this out, I'll lose her, and she's a long-term client. It'll cost me a fortune if I don't do something."

This already sounded far too complicated, but I was more concerned about her agitation. "Just calm down, Val. Tell me about it."

"It's too complicated. I need to show you, not just tell you. Can I come over? I'll pay whatever you ask, but I need someone to help me. Please."

When she said 'pay whatever you ask' I wished I hadn't mentioned mates' rates, but even so, I didn't hesitate any longer. In the past, the word 'pay' would never hook me the way it did my husband, but with things as they were, it helped, and there were times when I worried that I was getting too much like Dennis used to be.

I was about to insist on more details, but at that

moment, the alert bleeped on my phone. "All right, Val. Dennis is calling for me, and I need to see to him. Get yourself over here and we'll talk about it. Bring me whatever evidence you have, but it's on the strict understanding that if there's any hint of criminal goings on, not from you, but from your client, obviously, we contact the police."

"You have my word on it. I know where you live. Number seventeen isn't it?"

"Bracken Close. It's off Moor Road, on the right as you climb out of town. You've been before but it's a while ago, so if you're straining to remember, look for our new Fiat Diablo in the drive. I'm sorry, Val, I'll have to see to Dennis."

"I'll be there in twenty minutes, half an hour."

With that, I cut the call and hurried into the house.

Every time I walked into that room, I wanted to cry. I would never describe Dennis as outstandingly handsome, but the man lying on that bed bore only a vague, superficial resemblance to the tall, well-kept individual I had married. A month or more from The Incident, he had lost weight, but suffered a paradoxical increase in his waistline. It was easy to explain. He did a heavy job of work which kept him fittish, and despite having the appetite of a Grand National favourite, that helped keep him in trim. Now, he was doing nothing, and he wasn't eating as he used to. He couldn't. So while his overall weight went down, his abdominal muscles wasted and his belly grew a few inches.

The attack had done considerable damage. Both legs were broken; one of the right shin bones and his left thigh bone. They were mending, but he needed his legs raised at intervals to prevent swelling, and thanks to the McCruddens, the same couple who supplied the wheelchair accessible Diablo parked outside the house, we had a proper hospital bed in the spare room.

Again with the help of the McCruddens, who were partly responsible for his condition, we had spent a small fortune making alterations to the house; disabled aids in the toilet and shower, wheelchair ramps at side and conservatory doors and one from the decking to the garden. We had two wheelchairs, a manual, push-along type for use in the house, and a power wheelchair for when we had to go out. Again, both had been supplied by Keith and Eileen McCrudden, along with the Fiat Diablo. They also paid for the nurse's visits and as his legs mended, they would arrange physio for him.

His worst injury was a depressed skull fracture. He needed surgery to lift the fragments, and he now wore a padded skull helmet to protect the injury. Wasn't there once a goalkeeper in the football Premier League who used to wear one?

Thanks to that injury, his memory was hazy at the best of times. He had had to relearn who he was, who I was, who Simon, Naomi, Bethany (our granddaughter) were, and who Cappy the Cat was, but he had no recollection of The Incident, and of his life prior to that terrible night he had only flashes of memory. He had worked with Tony Wharrier and Greg Vetch for almost forty years, but he barely recognised either of them, and the workshop at Haxford Fixers where he spent anything up to sixty hours a week, was an alien environment to him.

There were, of course, other problems. His speech was slurred, often unintelligible, and over the past five weeks, I'd had to teach myself to interpret his words. His coordination was poor, and most noticeable at meal times. Most of the time he fed himself with a spoon, but he made a bigger mess than Bethany, and often, when he needed the toilet, he didn't make it. We kept him in disposable, incontinence pants which someone had to change at regular intervals, and we all know who that someone was, don't we? And I was out of practice. I hadn't dealt with so much nappy changing since Ingrid was a baby.

I had to help him dress and undress, and when we had to go to the hospital, I had to get him out of the house, into the power wheelchair, which we kept in the garage, so he could guide himself into the back of the Diablo.

And most important, whenever he called, such as he did while I was talking to Val, I had to go to him.

When I came into the room, he gave me a crooked smile. "Oil it," he croaked.

Given his lifelong work as a mechanic, anyone could be forgiven for thinking that his memory was wandering again, but sufficient time had passed for me to interpret it properly. He needed the toilet, or in his case, the commode.

Over the years there had been many occasions when I chose to undress him, most of them when he was drunk or we were getting, er, excited. Now it was not a pleasure, but an unpleasant necessity, a chore made worse when I had to change his incontinence underwear. But you do it, don't you? It's a part of that rich tapestry we call marriage.

Once I had him sorted out, cleaned up, dressed and in his wheelchair, I pushed him through to the kitchen, where I prepared him a bowl of cornflakes, and a cup of tea (served in a child's lidded, non-spill, plastic cup) and left him to it. Thankfully, he did not need feeding, merely cleaning up after he'd eaten, all of which I attended to, and hung his phone on the arm of his wheelchair so he could call me if and when he needed me.

I was going to sit him outside, but a quick glance at the clock told me Val was due any time now, and I still hadn't changed.

It was necessary. I would never receive visitors or clients in those shorts and that top. For one thing, the shorts were far too tight. Bend a little too quickly, and the sound of tearing would herald an unplanned display of tomorrow's laundry. Apart from that, my appearance was anything but professional, and as a professional, I insisted upon a professional appearance when meeting clients. Even those I knew. But it was far too hot for a business suit, so I chose a short skirt – but not too short – and a thin blouse in pale cream which I hoped would combat the heat.

I'd barely buttoned up my blouse when the doorbell rang, and I hurried along to greet her.

I instantly regretted having changed my outfit. She sported a short tank top and a pair of salmon pink shorts which showed off her rugby forward's thighs and enormous bottom. She had the bosom to match, and I felt that if my top half was that big, I'd have terrible backache carrying it around. To match her appearance all I really needed was a change of shorts, and I did have others which were not quite so bum-hugging as the ones I'd just taken off.

She was not unlovely. In her own way, she was quite a good-looking woman. It was just that there was so much of her. She had a shower of blonde-ish hair, a smooth, seductive voice, and a warm smile of welcome on her small mouth, but I knew that smile could turn to a throaty and alluring laugh when she was amused by something. And I thought Tony might have been having an affair? Her appearance confirmed my earlier notion that Val was the more likely candidate for a spot of extra-marital exercise.

All of which was absolutely nothing to do with me and nor was it part of the reason for her visit.

She was carrying a laptop bag when she greeted me with a smile and hug, and I ushered her through to the kitchen, where she fussed over Dennis for a minute (he hadn't a clue who she was) and settled her into the conservatory while I made coffee for us.

At length, I wheeled Dennis through the conservatory and out into the back garden where he could enjoy the sun, and sat with Val enjoying a cup of fresh coffee through the customary small talk. Like us, Val and Tony had two children, but theirs were two boys, Craig, twenty three, and Rodney, eighteen, so the chatter was predictable. How was Dennis, how were Simon, Naomi and Bethany, how was Ingrid, fine considering his infirmities, and the kids were fine. How was Tony, how were Craig and Rod faring, okay, okay, okay. Eventually, while watching Cappy the Cat trying to strike out a couple of sparrows attacking the suspended bird feeder in the garden, I brought us round to business, but first, I established my terms.

"I don't charge for the initial consultation, Val, but beyond that, my charges are now forty pounds an hour plus out of pocket expenses. Because we're friends, I'll cut that to twenty pounds an hour. That's assuming you'll want me to go further, but on that score, I can't guarantee to make any enquiries until I know what we're dealing with. How does that sound?"

"Fine." She picked up her laptop bag. "Mind if I plug this in?"

I agreed and dug out a large placemat of thick, woven straw to stand her laptop on. She plugged it into the mains and switched the machine on, and as she waited for it to come alive, she took another mouthful of coffee, settled back in her seat, and looked me in the eye.

"What I'm going to show you is highly confidential, Chrissy. It's not yet published and the writer has given me nothing but grief over it since last night. I'm struggling to persuade her that the police picking her up was nothing to do with me, and if she knew I was showing it to someone else, she'd hit the ceiling. I'd never hear from her again, and that would cost me a fair bit of money."

"No problem, Val. No names, no pack drill is my policy on the vlog and it's part and parcel of my efforts as a private eye."

"Good. Do you know what I do for a living?"

"I, er, well, according to Tony, you're a book critic or something." It wasn't actually Tony who told me. It was Dennis after Tony had told him, but with my husband, if he wasn't talking to an automotive design engineer, he didn't bother with trivia like paying attention. If you told him you were a trapeze artist, he'd insist you'd told him you were a skydiving specialist.

Val clucked. "Typical Tony. Honestly. Men. Only listen to half the tale and then get it wrong? Do you have the same trouble with Dennis?"

"Now and again," I admitted. It was better than telling her the truth. Even before The Incident, he didn't listen. Now, I was wasting my time talking to him most of the time, but according to the medics, it was necessary.

"And again, I'm so sorry for what happened to him," Val said when I explained this to her. "Tony stills feels it, you know. He's said all along that if he and Lester hadn't left early that night it wouldn't have happened."

I had to disagree. "Yes it would. It just wouldn't have happened then. Anyway, never mind Dennis and The Incident. You were telling me about the way you make your living."

"I'm a proof-reader and editor," she told me. "I'm properly trained and a member of a recognised society. I work exclusively with fiction, and I have a number of good, midlist authors on my books. I'm not cheap, but I'm not expensive either, and I believe I do a good job."

"Ah. Right. Interesting." It actually sounded as

boring as Tony's stamp collecting and vintage postcards, but my life was hardly the pinnacle of excitement as daydreams about Bloomy and Deppy would confirm.

"Do you read much, Chrissy?"

"I go through phases. I can read and read and read, and then I forget books for long enough." This was almost true. I did have the Kindle app on my smartphone and I loved the odd Agatha Christie or Caroline (Midsomer Murders) Graham, but most of the time, I read magazines like *Yours* or *Woman's Own*.

"Ever read anything by Anita Stocker?"

With a name like Stocker I had to wonder what she stocked, but Val was waiting for an answer. "Sorry. No. Is that her real name?"

"I, er, no. it's a pen name. Her real name is Janet Duckett, that's D-U-C-K-E-T-T. I usually refer to her as Anita. Does it matter?"

"No. Not really. Just gathering background information." When it came to that kind of lie, I was excellent. And with a real name like Duckett, I could understand why the woman needed a nom-de-plume. At the same time, the name, Duckett, not Stocker, rang a distant bell with me, but I couldn't place it. "So go on. What about her."

"She's very successful," Val said. "In fact, she's brilliant. A genuine creative genius. Mesmerising. Really compelling, draws you into her novels. Self-publishes everything through various web platforms. E-books mainly, like those you read on your Kindle app, but also puts out her work in paperback form. A lot of writers do it, these days, especially for hard-boiled crime fiction, and she makes more than a cheese and chutney sandwich out of the job." Val faffed about on the laptop for a moment. I couldn't see what she was doing, but it involved a bit of work with the mouse before she turned the machine to me. "It's quite strong stuff. She doesn't pull any punches, but do me a favour and read the passage I've marked, Chrissy."

It ran to about three hundred words from a much longer document, and it was revolting. It involved the murder of a woman in woodland. She was stabbed to death, stripped, left naked, and the killer used the murder weapon to cut out her eyes and carve pagan markings on her face and chest.

I understood that such things happened in real life – for God's sake, look at Dennis – but I could happily live without this kind of lurid and detailed description in fiction. The word processing package indicated that this was page ten of ten which I took to indicate that the document was a single chapter. If the remainder of the book was written in the same vein, I'd settle for Maigret.

Still, distressing as it was, I felt it was strangely familiar.

I turned the computer back without comment. Val spent another moment or two tippy-tapping on the keyboard, then pushed it back to me.

"Now check that out."

It was a web page from the previous evening's Haxford Recorder and it concerned the naked body of a woman, twenty-seven year old Fay Selkirk, found in Hattersley Woods. She had been stabbed to death, her eyes were cut out and the killer had carved what the police assumed were pagan markings all over her face.

No wonder Anita Stocker's book was familiar. I read about it the previous evening, but with Dennis always at the forefront of my mind, I tended to forget horrifying trivia like that.

"It's a copycat killing," I said. "The killer has obviously read Ms Stocker's book and he's copying the murderer."

Val shook her head. "That's not possible. The book isn't published yet, and Anita only sent me this chapter yesterday afternoon… less than an hour before the body of this woman was discovered in Hattersley Woods."

Chapter Three

Back in the days before The Incident, Dennis had this uncanny knack of interrupting at the most inconvenient times, usually with a phone call. He did it now, but obviously not by talking into the phone. Instead, his alert bleeped for attention.

As it happened, it was anything but inconvenient. I needed some time to think about the things Val told me. I checked the phone, and made my excuses. "I'm sorry, Val. I'll have to see to Dennis. He may need the smallest room and if so it could take a little while. Would you like to make us fresh coffee?"

"Sure. No problem."

She took our cups back to the kitchen to refresh the coffee, and I made my way out into the garden to check on Dennis.

There didn't appear to be anything amiss, but his head was lolling forward and the plastic cup dangled from his hand dangerously close to dropping to the lawn. He looked up when I tapped him gently on the wrist.

"Tired."

It didn't sound like 'tired'. It could have been 'hired', 'wired', or even 'fired' but none of them fitted.

"You want to go back to bed?"

He gave me a lopsided smile and nodded.

If there is a positive to having a husband suddenly become disabled and dependent, it's the capacity for bodybuilding. As if getting Dennis in and out of bed hadn't already taxed my trim, shapely little frame (it does have a shape. Not exactly an hourglass, but definitely feminine) the prospect of having to push the wheelchair with him in it back up the ramp and into the house, was enough to have your average athlete running for the changing room. I'd had a month of practice, and I now had leg muscles in parts of my legs that I didn't know existed.

It was particularly bad behind the conservatory and off the decking where the ramp had to rise something like nine inches in the space of about six feet. As far as I could calculate, that was a gradient of about one in eight. Our precious Fiat Diablo would need to be in first gear to make such a climb, but I wasn't fitted with a gearbox. All I had was raw strength, and before The Incident, I left such demanding tasks to Dennis.

There was an art to it. First, I would line the wheelchair up, then stare at the ramp, back to the back of Dennis's head, and then at the ramp again, psyching myself up for those few seconds of exhaustive exercise. It worked, but in the very early days, not long after he came home from hospital, the wheelchair wandered off to one side, and fell off the ramp, taking Dennis with it. It was fortunate that his speech was impeded. I dread to think what the language would have been like had he been able to express himself clearly.

Worse than all that, once I had him on the decking, I had it all to do again to get him into the conservatory.

I had perfected my technique, but it took Val by surprise when I ran at the ramp, and the wheelchair, Dennis, and me came hurtling back into the conservatory, where I had to bring it to a stop before it collided with the kitchen door.

"I would have helped," she said.

"It's all right, thanks, Val. I'm getting the hang of it these days. Dennis is nodding off, and I need to get him back into bed. Just give me a few minutes."

Carrying a hand towel to wipe the sweat from my face and arms, I joined her about ten minutes later. That interval gave me time to consider her problem. I didn't know all the ins and outs, but there were only two obvious conclusions.

Val spoke of Anita Stocker has someone of importance, and she'd admitted that she made a fair amount of money from the woman, but the obvious occurred to me right away. Ms Stocker had seen the piece in the Recorder and copied it into her book. I'd never even met the woman, but she was obviously not the creative genius Val made her out to be. Given the inclination, I daresay I could have turned out this kind of trashy, pulp fiction based on newspaper reports of real, gruesome murders.

Not that I would. My blogs and vlogs were factual with a healthy dose of uplifting opinion and humour thrown in to generate good cheer. And anyway, if I ever considered writing fiction, it would be romance, with rugged, handsome men forging a future on a sun-baked, deserted island, eyeing up startlingly buxom wenches who might look a lot like me.

Beyond that, the only other explanation was that Anita Stocker had committed the murder in Hattersley Woods and then put it in her book. Why else would the police have questioned her?

With my mind already made up, having solved the 'murder' I could enjoy a second cup of coffee while bringing Mrs Wharrier back down to earth with a few gentle home truths about her genuine, creative genius of a novelist. I supplied a small plate of Rich Tea biscuits, which Val declined (perhaps she needed to skip the snacks in order to get her bulky frame down one dress size) and joined her.

I was about to launch into my analysis when Val spoke first.

"Now I know what you're thinking," she said and I wondered where I'd heard that line before. I think it was from a Clint Eastwood movie, but I couldn't say which one. When Clint was on the telly, I didn't always focus on the dialogue. "You're thinking that Anita read the piece in the Recorder and copied the details as the opening shot in her new novel."

"It did occur to me," I agreed while nibbling a Rich Tea. CutCost were out of McVities, and I'd had to settle for own label cheapies. With that in mind, I was glad Val refused. With Dennis's income cut in half, I couldn't bear the thought of her feeling sorry for me.

"Not possible."

Val moved to sit alongside me, shifted her coffee

to a position where she could comfortably reach it, and brought the laptop round so we could both concentrate on the screen. Once ready, she opened the document, which I noticed was named *'uttcar'* – which I guessed was a mnemonic to help Anita recall the file – and began to point out the periphery. It had been produced using Microsoft Word, a package I was completely at home with because I used it for preparing my blogs posts and the scripts for my vlogs.

Val pointed along the bottom of the screen, the grey area where I had first noticed the number of pages. Alongside the second item I read, 'Words: 3107'.

"Over three thousand words," Val said, "and although there are some spelling queries, they're likely to be non-standard English names or slang terms which are not in the local software's dictionary."

She moved to the file options and called up the document properties. Before she pointed it out, I knew where she was going. Uttcar was created at six the previous evening, which was presumably when Val received it.

She did exactly as I believed she would, and said, "Those times are not definitive. I don't know how much comes from my machine when I first downloaded the file. But the Recorder only reported that murder in Hattersley Woods at five yesterday afternoon, and the police are speculating that the victim was killed less than three hours previously. Think about it, Chrissy. Could you create and type over three thousand words in less than an hour, proofread it, spellcheck it – and I don't just mean using the software's spellchecker – and package it off to me in so short a time?"

Val's forcefulness was beginning to get to me, along with the cheap biscuits. Who was the consultant here? Her or me? I was the super sleuth, not her. Deductions like that were my department.

In order to bring her down a peg or to, I agreed, but qualified my agreement. "It's unlikely, but not impossible. A professional typist can hit speeds of up to eighty words a minute, and that entire document—" I waved at the screen "— could be no more than forty minutes' work." I pressed on before she could interrupt further. "However, as I said, it's unlikely, but it does leave you, or us, with a more disturbing possibility, doesn't it?"

"That Anita murdered the poor girl in Hattersley Woods." Val did not phrase it as a question, demonstrating once again that she had anticipated me. When I nodded she went on. "I won't have it. I've known her a long time, Chrissy. She is an irritable, middle-aged, but highly focussed woman, and although she can be quite forceful, she wouldn't hurt the proverbial fly."

"Do you know how many such unlikely murderers are behind bars, Val? Men and women who would go out of their way to help an injured pigeon, but were absolutely evil when it came to shuffling others off their mortal coil? Haigh was like that, wasn't he? And he got rid of his victims in baths of acid. I'm sorry, Val, but that is the alternative."

She looked away to where a couple of pigeons

were locked in combat with a brace of magpies picking over the lawn and Cappy the Cat scurrying round to chase them off. When she looked back, it was with a face lined in pain. "And the police have already questioned her. Someone rang them yesterday evening, insisting that he – or she – had read this murder in one of Anita Stocker's books. The caller didn't give a name, but the police acted immediately. Paddy Quinn led the interrogation."

I maintained my equilibrium. Until The Incident Paddy Quinn and I got on like John Wayne and Apache braves, but ever since that night, he had treated me with unaccustomed gentility. "It's par for the course," I responded.

"They released Anita late last night, and when she got home, she rang me, screaming down the phone, insisting that I had rung the police. I didn't, and by the time I managed to get that message across, she was insisting that I'd shown her manuscript to someone else, and that someone rang the police. It didn't happen, Chrissy. I wouldn't do that. She's threatening to drop me as her editor, and frankly, I can't afford to lose her. She knocks out three or four books a year and as well as my editing fees, I also pick up commission from sales resulting from my publicity efforts. If she drops me, I'll lose a flaming fortune… Well, maybe not a fortune, but a sizeable slice of my annual income. Not only that, but she has a significant web presence and she'd be sure to let everyone know that I'd sold her out. Writers would avoid me like they avoided people not wearing facemasks when covid was at its peak. There must be another way."

I sympathised. Well, I would, wouldn't I? There were a number of small businesses in Haxford which sponsored my vlog, but if I criticised even one of them, not only would I lose the sponsor in question, but every other business in the town. I didn't make a lot of money from them but it still came to more than I could afford to lose.

"Is she a Haxforder?" I asked.

"Hilly Farm," she told me, and my idiotic mind put together the farm and Duckett, the lady's real name, generating an absurd vision of Hilltop Farm in the Lake District which had been owned by Beatrix Potter, creator of Jemima Puddleduck. Janet Duckett – Jemima Puddleduck?

"Could we go to see her? Talk to her in person?"

Doubt spread across Val's face. "She's very private. And there's nothing to say that she won't lose the plot and fire me if we did."

"All right. Could I go alone?"

There was no doubt this time. Val was quite firm on the matter. "And how would you explain having seen this chapter from her next book? These things are confidential, Chrissy. Aside from me, nobody, absolutely nobody sees them until the books are finished, and even then it's only a few chosen, specialist readers who see them prior to publication." She delivered a thin smile. "They critique them and Anita uses the comments for her publicity after publication."

It was problematic. In order to let my brain freewheel on the matter, I posed an irrelevant question. "How come she only sends you one chapter? Why doesn't she wait until the book is written and then send you the entire thing?"

"Guidance," Val explained. "She roughs out a plot and asks my opinion. I give her a yea or a nay, and she goes from there. She then writes the first chapter and sends it to me, asking me to assess it for tone and content, and I make recommendations from there. I don't hear anything then for a couple of months before I get the full script, and that's when my real work begins."

Still trying to think of an excuse to get her to come with me to see the writer, I diverted her attention again. "Have you been doing this long, Val?"

"Virtually since I left school. I worked for a publishing company in Leeds. Mainly text books and what have you, but I gave it up when Tony and I got married and the boys came along. I became a stay at home mum, and you know what that's like. You gave up the police when Simon and Ingrid were born, didn't you?"

"I did. Boring doesn't come into it. I tried a few part time jobs, but they were almost as bad. And then the internet came along and I started blogging and vlogging. At least I can carry on doing that while I'm looking after Dennis."

"It was the same with me, and it was down to the internet, too. With the arrival of e-books and self-publishing, I took a chance, paid for a training course in proofreading and editing and set myself up. Anita was one of my first clients. She's important to me. I need someone to help me prove that I didn't ring the police and I didn't show this script to anyone."

I had been in this situation many times. Well, not many times but certainly more than my fair share. People confronted with the reality that they did not want to confront.

"You have to be sensible about this, Val. Nobody knows Paddy Quinn better than me, and I know he can be hasty, but if the police say they had a tipoff, then it's guaranteed that they did. Who apart from you could possibly have seen this manuscript?"

"Anita insists no one, and that's what I have to persuade her of. I swear to you it wasn't me. I thought if you could investigate, and find out who it was, then at least it would clear me, and Anita and I could go back to the way we were, the way we're supposed to be: editor and client."

"That won't be easy. You say she's a Haxforder?" I waited for Val to nod. "Then why don't we go and see her?"

She was hesitant. "Well, like I said, she's very private and she might not take too kindly to our asking."

"Then we don't ask. We just turn up and ring the doorbell."

"That could lead to confrontation."

I sighed, forcing patience upon myself. "That's inevitable, Val. There will be a confrontation, and as always, I can't offer any guarantees as to how it will turn out, but it is the only way, and let's face it, it's not as if I'm asking you to go alone, is it? I'll be there, and I don't know this woman. Trust me, I can handle her."

"But what about Dennis?"

I recognised this objection for what it was; a last desperate attempt to avoid the inevitable. "I'll ask Mrs McQuarrie from next door to come and sit in for a couple of hours. I do her shopping for her, and she doesn't mind."

At last, Val capitulated. "All right. If you insist."

Chapter Four

Hazel McQuarrie was a seventy-seven-year-old widow. Her husband passed away about three years ago. We had been neighbours ever since Dennis and I moved into number seventeen, almost thirty years previously, when we were sprightly twenty-somethings, and she and her husband, Arnold were in their mid-to-late forties. She had watched us mature from young, inexperienced parents to settled middle-age, watched our children grow from babies through toddlers, through cheeky children, insouciant teenagers, to well-rounded adults, and over the years Hazel and I had been not exactly friends, but good neighbours.

Her son and two daughters were all resident in Leeds or Manchester or York; certainly somewhere other than Haxford, and according to Hazel, they frequently pestered her to sell up and move in with one or other of them. An independent woman, she steadfastly refused, and The Incident had given her firm ground upon which to stand.

"Christine needs me to help with Dennis," she told them. "I couldn't possibly leave Bracken Close now."

When we first met, she was a ward nurse at Haxford Cottage Hospital, later a practice nurse with a GP. Her background proved useful when Dennis first came home, and I didn't have to ask. She volunteered.

"If you need a break, Christine, give me a shout. I'll look after him for a few hours."

It didn't happen often. Most of the time, Naomi would come and stay with him, but she wasn't always available and anyway, it was clear from her reticence, that she didn't care for the close attention Dennis often needed; the business of helping him wash, change his clothing and underwear. Hazel had no problem.

"Seen it all and done it all before, luv." That was her attitude.

When I rang her, she was quite happy to come round even though I told her I was likely to be a couple of hours.

"I've nowt better to do, lass. Give me a few minutes, and I'll come round."

We had always had an understanding that if she needed bits of shopping, I would pick it up while I was out. Since The Incident, I had done my weekly shop online. It saved me having to leave Dennis for the two-hour drudge at the supermarket, and CutCost's delivery charges were quite reasonable. Given the price of petrol, it didn't cost much more. And it was Hazel who gave me the idea. An intelligent, internet familiar woman with all her marbles in place, she struggled to get about on a crumbling hip, and she'd been having her weekly shop delivered for ages. I tried it, liked the system, and although there were times when I missed getting out to the supermarket, it solved a major headache for me without having to rely on Simon and Naomi.

A small, slightly overweight woman, since The Incident I'd noticed that her limp was getting worse, and when she came into the house, I asked after the problem.

"It's just about gone, Chrissy. I'm due in Huddersfield Royal any time soon for a hip replacement. In fact, I was going to ask you if you can watch out for me when I come out. Assuming Dennis is all right, of course."

"You know you only have to ask, Hazel. Now, are you sure you'll be all right while Val and I are out?"

"Go on. Get yourselves out. Go get drunk if you feel like it. Heaven knows, you deserve it, the trouble you've had recently."

"It's business, not pleasure. Dennis is asleep right now and I don't know where Cappy the Cat is."

"He'll come back when he's hungry. You get going. Get your business sorted out."

We elected to take Val's car since it was a) possessed of a larger engine which would handle the hills better, and b) it had air conditioning, vital in the increasing heat of the day. All my Diablo had was an up-and-down sun roof, and even that had to be operated by hand.

Most of the farms around Haxford were on the moors. That's because the town was surrounded by moors. The farms were also on top of hills. Again it was obvious since Haxford sat in a deep valley, surrounded on all sides by hills. The road to

Huddersfield was the only way out of town that was anything like level. If you were following any other road, it was uphill.

Hilly Farm was no exception. It was two miles to the west of town, and was anything but hilly. It sat in the middle of a moorland plateau and I guessed it was so named to identify it for postmen, delivery drivers, satellite TV salesmen, and other pains in the bottom. If it had been called Hill Farm everyone would ask which farm on which hill, but the addition of a letter 'y' on the first part of the name was enough to pinpoint it.

It was no longer a farm, and once again, this was a common situation. Haxford was part of what had once been known as the Heavy Woollen District, and we specialised in sheep farming. The advent of manmade fibres signed the death knell of keeping sheep other than for meat and livestock shows, and while most of the outlying places tended and grazed their flocks on the moors, mutton no longer outnumbered people, and livestock shows didn't happen every other day. That was an arbitrary assumption on my part. There were about 25,000 people in Haxford at the last census, and I'm sure there were not that many sheep, but I don't think anyone had ever actually counted them.

Whatever its part in the history of Haxford, Hilly Farm no longer fulfilled that role. Instead it stood in grand isolation on a flat plain, with spectacular views of the tall transmitters of Emley Moor to the east and Holme Moss to the west, and it served, according to Val, as Anita Stocker's home for eight months of the year. She passed the remaining four months from the beginning of November to the end of February living as Janet Duckett at her apartment in Benalmedena on the Costa del Sol.

When Val told me this, I came to the reluctant conclusion that notwithstanding his injuries, Dennis and I were in the wrong jobs. The writers of such gruesome fiction obviously earned a lot more than I imagined.

"It depends how they approach the job," Val told me as she negotiated the steep and twisting Hilly Lane which took us out of Haxford. "Anita does a lot of advertising all over the web. It costs a pretty penny but it doesn't half bring in results. There are times when she's selling hundreds of books a day. Just to underscore this point, I have a couple of writers on my books who refuse to invest in advertising and they sell a dozen books a week."

"She's aiming for her first million?" I suggested.

"I don't say she's that well off, but the apartment in Spain cost the better part of two hundred thousand. Mind, some of that came from her husband's life insurance. He was insured for about a hundred k when he clocked out."

"Must have been an executive of some kind, then?" I said.

"Actually, he was mechanic. Ran a small business. Duckett's Auto Repairs. Like Dennis's. In fact, I believe Dennis and Tony both knew him. I know Tony did."

It was news to me. I'm sure I would have remembered if Dennis had mentioned someone by the name of Duckett. "And how did he die?"

There must have been a hint of suspicion in my

voice because Val laughed as we reached the plateau and Hilly Farm appeared off to the left, half a mile ahead of us, a little white dot in the wilderness.

"Tony sounded just as suspicious as you when he heard about it, but it was an accident. It's ten years ago, now. Maybe more. He was working under a car. He had it raised on one of those hydraulic lift thingies, and it collapsed. He was crushed under it." Her face darkened. "He wasn't old, either. Only about sixty."

Despite her insistence that there was nothing suspicious about Mr Duckett's death, I was with Tony, and I made a mental note to look into it when I got home. If Val had the tale right, and my husband knew Duckett, he would also know all about the poor man's demise... if I could get the information out of him. Not that I could see it having any bearing on our business, but history of this kind often proved useful when you needed to turn the screws, put pressure on a witness... or a suspect.

We turned off the lane and onto the rough, one-hundred-yard track leading to the house, which looked like any other moorland farm to me. Surrounded by a drystone wall, a scrub of grass out front, two cars, one a late model Range Rover with personalised number plates the other a sporty, nearly new Volvo, no sign of life around the place or through the double-glazed windows. There wasn't even a washing line. Maybe wealthy authors didn't do laundry. Maybe they sent their dirty clothing to charity shops and bought new every week. Alternatively, it could be at the back of the house, which from the general aspect faced roughly southwest and would get more sun to help the washing dry quicker.

Val stopped behind the Range Rover and a wall of raw heat hit me the moment I climbed out of the car. There was not a breath of wind, and as I took in the scenic view, looking southeast in the general direction of Sheffield, the horizon shimmered. I was glad of the minimal shade afforded by the porch where Val rang the bell.

"Sebastian will answer," she told me. "Anita's son."

After a slight delay, the door opened and I was confronted with a fitness fanatic... all right so that was an assumption, but his physique backed it. About thirty years old, dark hair mussed around his head, a square jaw and brown eyes that burned with energy, the rest of him matched that fire and energy. He wore a pair of shorts and a running vest which exposed his athletic calves, well-developed biceps and sinewy wrists, and the immediate impression I had was of a poseur, which I think said more about my attitude to this kind of person. Other than the occasional passing fancy, and even that was more about my personality, I had no interest in beefcake. Despite the meandering of my mind all morning, dreaming of Bloomy and Deppy, I preferred everyone to know that I was married and not a target for men like this who, if I assessed him correctly, indulged a narcissistic approach to his looks and plied his (theoretical) charm on available females. Hadn't Ossie Travis been of the same mould?

In this instance I was further put off by a look of not exactly thunder, but irritation in his eyes. At first I thought it might be my imagination but the moment he spoke, it was confirmed.

"Not a wise move, Valerie. You're persona non grata right now." He sounded well educated; enunciation perfect, accent anywhere but Haxford.

Val's face sank and I had to take the initiative. I took half a pace forward. "Allow me to introduce myself. Christine Capper, private investigator."

"And you're not likely to be welcome, either."

"Which doesn't trouble me as much as it does Mrs Wharrier because I'm used to it. Valerie is my client and I'm here to see if we can clear up the confusion. She's been accused of something she hasn't done."

"You say."

"I do, but one way or the other, Mr Duckett—"

"I prefer Stocker."

"Whereas, I prefer reality and I doubt that you were christened with your mother's pen name. As I was saying, whether Val is guilty or innocent, I will prove it."

And he smiled. He actually smiled and it threw me off guard slightly. "The Miss Marple of Haxford." He offered his hand. "Sebastian Stocker. Most people call me Seb."

We shook hands and I noticed the skin was soft, gentle to the touch. He'd obviously never done what Dennis would call a proper day's work in his life.

"I wouldn't expect a warm welcome, Mrs Capper," Sebastian went on. "Mother is absolutely furious. She spent several hours at the police station yesterday evening after someone rang them."

"I've been made aware of the situation, Sebastian, and it seems your mother blames Valerie. If she'll speak to me, not only will I clear Val's name, but I should be able to identify the source of the, er, leak."

He stood back to let us in, closed the door behind us, and led the way to the, well, I suppose one could call it the living room.

"Mum, we have visitors."

'Mum'? That was a rarity in Haxford. Most people used 'Mam'. Perhaps Duckett the younger really had been better educated, although, on second thoughts, that was no benchmark. My son, Simon, spent three years at university and he still called me Mam.

Dismissing the pointless speculation, I looked around. This place was the last word in luxury. I swear I had seen that pure white, three seater sofa on one of those late evening chat programmes where the guest were all top drawer celebrities who wouldn't sit on anything cheaper. And I didn't know where the mahogany occasional table and matching display unit came from, but it wasn't Ikea. At the front of the room, the old fireplace had been ripped out, bricked up and plastered over, and an ornate fake put in its place. It was all white with gold, inlaid braiding, and in the centre sat a coal-effect electric convector heater. Hung on the wall to one side of the fireplace was a humongous TV screen. I swear that the last time I saw a screen that large I was at the cinema. Watching *Strictly Come*

Dancing on that would be like having a front seat in Blackpool Tower Ballroom.

Anita Stocker or Janet Duckett, whatever she liked to call herself, was perched in a fireside armchair, legs curled under her, reading something on an iPad until her son disturbed her, when she put down the iPad, stood up and faced us.

I remembered watching a TV programme once where they interviewed a well-known romance author, a woman who spent her life dreaming up tales of drop-dead gorgeous young women seduced and entranced by handsome hunks like Ossie Travis and Sebastian Duckett, and yet the author was about fifty years old and weighed in at around seventeen stones.

That memory came back to me and I had anticipated Anita Janet Duckett Stocker as something similar.

I gave myself a silent round of applause for having got it so wrong.

She was about my age, early fifties. The resemblance ended there. I made an effort to look after myself but I was not in this woman's league. About my height (a dainty five feet four) she cut a trim, shapely figure, poured into a skin-tight, thigh-length, taupe coloured dress. Strong, powerful legs, the kind men liked to drool over, complemented by a well-developed (or well-packed chest) and a carefully coiffeured head of dark hair. Her face, too, could have been pretty, but there was a set about her mouth and a dangerous gleam in her dark eyes which looked at the world, decided it was not good enough and if it didn't change, there would be repercussions.

And right now, most of the nuclear threat was aimed at Val and me. "What the hell are you doing here?" The demand was aimed at Val, but it didn't take long for the acid to turn on me. "I don't know who you are, and I don't care. Get out. Both of you."

Taking into account the strain I'd been under for the last months, it would have been so easy for me to lose my temper, but I held it.

"Do you greet all visitors like that, Mrs Puddleduck?" It was a not so deliberate error on my part. With Hilltop Farm on the brain I began with 'Pudd...' and was about to trail off but instead I went on to add '...leduck' just to annoy her even further. And it worked, but before she could slide into full rant mode, I pressed on. "I do beg your pardon. Mrs Duckett, I am a former police officer turned private investigator, and Valerie called me because she was concerned over the startling accusations you've levelled against her."

Anita did not appear put out by my candour. She aimed a shaking finger at Val. "Thanks to her and her big mouth, I spent several hours at Haxford police station yesterday, interrogated by some moron call Quinn. Someone tipped them off that the murder in Hattersley Woods mirrored the opening chapter of Utter Carnage, which is my next novel, and the only one who could possibly know that is her."

Once again I stood my ground. At least I knew what the file name 'uttcar' stood for. "Let's work on the assumption that you're right. I know you're not, but let's work on that principle. If Val rang the police, then she did the right thing. For her to do anything else would be considered withholding information relevant to a serious crime, and she could be prosecuted for it. Knowing Paddy Quinn as well as I do, I'm surprised he hasn't charged you. Or do I have that wrong? Has he charged you?"

Her anger showed no signs of calming. "He released me under investigation. Me. As if I would do something like that, or even sponsor that kind of crime. And she's the one who rang them."

For the first time, Val felt obliged to defend herself. "It was not me, Anita. Your work is confidential. I never repeat anything to anyone."

I cut in again, calmer this time, more amenable. "I'm here to help and advise, Mrs Stocker. Someone obviously has betrayed your creative secrets to the Haxford police. I was one of their number, and I still have friends at the station. If you're willing to listen, if you're willing to speak to me, I will have a word with them and see what I can learn. But one way or another, I will find out who was behind this business, I will clear Valerie's name, and if you carry on with this arrogant attitude, I will go public on the matter, leaving you to face the consequences of your false accusations."

She was still blazing. "Get out. Both of you."

I turned for the door, Val floundered, and rescue came from an unexpected source: Sebastian. "For crying out loud, mother, get off your high horse and listen to the woman before you wind up in even more trouble."

I knew he meant it. Calling her 'mother' was a

dead giveaway. The only time Simon ever referred to me as 'mother' was when I annoyed him.

Finding myself with an unexpected ally, I pressed home my point. "You must have realised the similarity between your opening chapter and the murder in Hattersley Woods, and that being the case, as matters stand, you're already guilty of withholding information, and I'm certain that Paddy will add obstructing the police in the course of their duties, he'll strengthen the withholding information charge to one of withholding evidence possibly relative to a serious crime, which could be construed as an attempt to pervert the course of justice. He may also decide that your work is promoting, perhaps encouraging violent crime, and possibly even aiding and abetting. And if I know Paddy Quinn, he'll come up with a few more."

I didn't know if half these charges were possible or even valid, but my diatribe had the desired effect. Even Sebastian looked doubtful. "Really?" he asked.

"I told you. I know him. He hates me, he hates most of his subordinates, and the only thing he hates more, are people, the general public... especially those with money who think they can do as they please. If you'll take some advice, Anita, Janet or whatever you choose to call yourself, talk to me as well as Valerie. I guarantee that as long as it's not criminal, whatever you say to me will go no further than this room and the people in it."

Sebastian turned pleading eyes on his mother. "Listen to her, Mum. Please."

She took a long time making up her mind. She

stared around the four walls, gazed on a photograph of a man I assumed was her husband, as if seeking inspiration, permission or simple agreement from him, and then at last, she looked first to Val, and then to me.

"All right."

Chapter Five

"Your husband is Dennis Capper. Yes?"

I nodded and Anita went on.

"I read about the attack on him. You're lucky."

Once she'd calmed down and seen the sense of her son's words, Anita (it was the name she preferred to be known by) led us out to the rear of the house where we spread ourselves around a glass-topped picnic table, and after Sebastian served up a pitcher of iced lemonade, she launched into a brief account of her widowhood.

She sat opposite Val and me, her legs crossed showing more thigh than would be good for Dennis's blood pressure, and I say that because out in the lawned, back garden (where I noticed she had a rotary washing line) we were surrounded by drystone walls, just like the front, and there was nothing remotely mechanical which would distract my old man. Given a David Brown tractor or some such farming vehicle nearby, Dennis would never have noticed those thighs, but without it, his eyes would be popping.

And I envied her legs. How dare she be as old as me and enjoy such a trim figure? Still, I suppose when money was no object, the outcome was a forgone conclusion.

But that did not give her the right to tell me I was 'lucky' and I bristled at the assertion. "Lucky? Dennis needs twenty-four-seven care. I have to wash and dress him, half the time he doesn't know who I am, and the rest of the time he doesn't know who he is. I feel anything but lucky."

Anita was unrepentant. "You still have a husband, and I'm sure he'll recover. Mine didn't. I'm a widow, Mrs Capper. A nasty accident at his workshop ten years ago, took him from me. But you should know about it. He knew Dennis, he knew Tony Wharrier. In fact, I think he taught them when they worked for Addison's. Men like them, all with the same trade, tend to gossip more than bored housewives." She went on with her story, casting a regal wave at the farmhouse. "His death settled the mortgage on this place and I sold off some of the adjoining land. He had a sizeable life policy, too, so overall, I was well set up. But money isn't everything, is it? I stared at these walls day in, day out, week in, week out, and then I remembered how I used to enjoy writing when I was younger, so I turned his tragic death into a tale of criminal revenge and when I couldn't find a publisher, I did it myself. Tablets like the Kindle had become popular about that time. I took a couple of marketing courses – online, of course – sank some money into advertising, and lo, I had a bestseller. But it attracted a lot of criticism, mainly for the poor editing. That's when I got in touch with Valerie, and she's been my editor ever since."

"It's always been a mutually beneficial arrangement, Anita," Val concurred.

"Indeed. Since then I've produced – I don't know – getting on for forty books. I find writing them very easy, and I target myself to produce three or four every year. As a natural consequence of that popularity, I had wannabe writers from all over the world asking me how to do it, so I set up training courses for them. For a couple of hundred pounds they get a solid introduction and instruction in not only writing but selling books. I'm sure some of them are doing well, others not so well, because ultimately, it's a symbiosis – for want of a better word – between writing and selling. The writing comes first. It has to be top drawer, or at least as close to that as a body can get. The selling is almost as important. Most writers call it 'marketing' and I suppose that's a more accurate description because you don't sell books the way you sell apples and potatoes on the local market. If you can't sell, if you don't know how to construct your ads, where and when to place them, your book will remain invisible, and no matter how well it's written, how good the story, you won't sell."

I could think of a range of objections to her final assertion, starting with High Street booksellers, but I had no doubt that she would come back with a series of rebuttals, the simplest of which was her lavish lifestyle and an apartment in Benalmadena. Whether or not she had analysed the situation accurately, she was a success.

Instead I concentrated on possible means by which someone could have come across the plot of *Utter Carnage*.

"You run these courses. During the sessions, do

you discuss plots of forthcoming novels?"

"Not in detail. I may touch upon them, but I don't go into detail."

"And the one currently in production? Utter Carnage, is it? How many people know about the plot?"

Anita sipped her lemonade while she thought about the question. "A fair few, but again, not in so much detail."

To my relief, she uncrossed her legs, put the glass down, leaned forward and aimed a slender finger into the table top.

"What's happened, Mrs Capper—"

"Christine, please. Or Chrissy, if you prefer."

"As you wish, Christine. What's happened is impossible... I take that back. It's not impossible, because it's happened, but there are only two or three possible explanations. One, I murdered that young woman, and I know for a fact, I didn't. Two, Valerie did it, but she didn't see that chapter until after the body turned up. Three, Valerie read about it and phoned the police the moment she saw this first chapter. That, Christine, is a breach of our confidentiality agreement."

"It wasn't me, Anita," Val pleaded.

To prevent another battle breaking out, I intervened. "There is another possible explanation, Anita. Someone has hacked your system and they're tracking, perhaps stealing everything you write."

At this point, Sebastian interrupted. "Not so. Mum's laptop is secure, and there is no trace of anyone hacking her or her emails."

I mirrored Anita's actions and took a long

draught from my glass. The thirst-quenching bite on my tongue and palate carried me back a couple of hours to my garden, Cappy the Cat snoozing close by, Bloomy and Deppy arguing over who would take me to heaven.

I had to force myself to concentrate on Anita's son. "You're an IT expert, are you, Sebastian?"

I don't know what he had in his glass, but it was more than lemonade. It had a pale ochre tint to it, and I suspected either brandy or whisky.

"Not an expert," he told us, "but I know where I'm at with computers. Mum employs top line antivirus and anti-malware software, and that machine is more secure than the town hall's."

Doubt cross my mind. It was all very well him saying he knew what he was doing, but computer security was a specialised field.

"So if you're not a qualified systems man, what do you do?"

"Security," he said, and left the explanation to his mother.

"Sebastian works for me, Christine. And I mean he works for me officially. He's paid a salary just like any other employee would be." She was at pains to stress the rationale. "Think about it. I live out here, the middle of nowhere. My location is no great secret, especially in Haxford, and it leaves me vulnerable to attack. Obviously, we have all the necessary alarms, and even security cameras, but even so, while Sebastian is here, no one would dare attack this house, no one would dare come anywhere near me."

The man in question smiled modestly and

deliberately flexed his right bicep. "I'm more than capable of handling myself in tight situations, Mrs Capper. Anyone trying to get to Mum has to get through me first."

A spurious thought leapt into my febrile mind. How would he react if a young woman tried to get to him rather than his mother? And I didn't mean me. At the side of Bloomy and Deppy he could take his biceps and...

It wasn't just the pointless wandering of a middle-aged woman's mind. Suppose someone decided to steal Anita's work? Could they use a honey trap to distract Sebastian? I put the idea to him in the form of an elliptical query. "You live here, obviously. You're unmarried?"

He laughed. "Still playing the field, and trust me, it's a large field and I get plenty of playtime."

My initial assessment of him was justified. Totally in love with himself.

He was still speaking. "But even when I'm out, Mum knows I'm only a phone call away. And when she floats off to the Costa del Sol every winter, I go with her. And, before you ask, I do take girlfriends with me... but not all the time. The Spanish Costas, see. Plenty of spare."

Anita took up the narrative, quelling my annoyance at her son's near misogyny. "My son is entitled to a life, Christine. He does live here, but not in the house. He has his own apartment here, and we have an understanding that when he decides to settle down, he and his wife can take the house and I'll move into the granny flat."

Sebastian laughed again. "But that won't be for a

few years yet."

I kept my thoughts to myself. The arrangement struck me as unnatural. A young man like this, an obvious babe magnet (cringe) still living with his mother. Simon left our nest at the age of eighteen to spend three years at Leeds University, and when he came back, he was with us less than a month before he found his own place. And he was only twenty-two at the time. Not long after that, he met Naomi and they bought their own place. With showbiz ambitions, Ingrid cleared off to Scarborough to work on a holiday park when she was eighteen and aside from occasional visits never came back. I was sad to see her leave, sad to see Simon fly the nest, but it was the way of things. For instance, I was twenty-four when I settled down to live with Dennis, but before that, I was living away from my parents.

Was I just being old-fashioned? I knew that modern couples were leaving the family nest later in life, so perhaps Sebastian living with his mother wasn't so strange after all.

It was left to Val, who had contributed very little to the debate, to bring us back on track. "I promise you, Anita, this had nothing to do with me, so we still don't know how anyone got to the script in order to phone the police. Perhaps the murder was just a coincidence."

I disagreed. "Highly unlikely. Judging from the brief extract I read of your next novel, Anita, the Hattersley Woods murder was an exact copy. Perhaps that's a little over the top. Your novel said 'pagan signs' on the face of the victim. You don't go into detail. The report in last night's Recorder said the same thing, and didn't go into detail, but that's likely because the police won't have released such details. Other than that, the descriptions were the same. Multiple stab wounds and the victim's eyes either cut or gouged out." I shuddered at the thought. "Forgive me. I don't normally read such graphic tales."

At my admission that I'd seen the offending chapter, some of Anita's irritation returned, but her response to my point was scathing. "Have you ever seen King Lear?" I nodded by return but that didn't stop her pressing on. "Cornwall stamps on one of Gloucester's eyes and gouges the other out. If I'm writing horrifying descriptions, Christine, I'm in good company. That kind of graphic savagery stretches back as far as Shakespeare, possibly further, and if we read and trust the lurid descriptions in the newspapers, my work can be described as realistic."

My reply was just as tart. "It wasn't a criticism. I was merely stating a personal preference." Another sip of chilled lemonade helped me calm down. "And to get back to what I was saying, the similarity between the real murder and your work is too close for it to be coincidence. Aside from you, your son, and Valerie, who else could possibly read your work?"

"No one."

"And your list is one person too long," Sebastian told me. "I don't read Mum's work. Not even when it's published. I prefer science fiction."

Anita smiled fondly upon him. "Star Wars, Lord

of the Rings, Harry Potter, Avengers."

I had the feeling that Simon was of the same disposition, but I couldn't be sure. It was a long time since he and I had talked about books and movies.

Once again, I brought my wandering thoughts to bear. "Nevertheless, although we have to accept the possibility of coincidence, it's remote, and we have to assume that someone, somewhere, has somehow managed to read your opening chapter and carried out the crime. And it's highly likely that the same someone rang the police. You mentioned training courses. Is it likely that any of them could have learned of the plot details?"

"It's possible, but I don't see how. Not in such detail anyway. I don't know these people and although I know where they say they live – anywhere and everywhere from Hull to Hong Kong, Manchester to Mumbai, Keighley to Kuala Lumpur – for all I know they could be lying about that, and it's a fair bet that more than one or two live in the Huddersfield-stroke-Haxford area, too. As I said, I'm quite well-known in these parts and that will attract more than a couple of local hangers-on."

"Not to mention trolls," Sebastian put in. He focussed on me. "A troll is—"

"Yes, thank you, Sebastian," I cut him off. "I'm familiar with the term and more than familiar with trolls."

When I first began vlogging, I picked up a couple of trolls, and one was persistent in the extreme. He kept pestering me for a date of all things. Despite my rebuffs, he would not go away and I eventually reported him to the site which hosts my vlog and they cut him off at the broadband. It was quite flattering in its own way, but for all I knew he could have been a twelve-year-old boy with a mummy fixation. I never told Dennis. He'd have asked whether the troll was in the market for a compact Hyundai.

Time was getting on and I decided it was time to bring matters to a close. "All right, Anita, let me tell you the situation. Someone told the police, and by rights, they needed to know." She opened her mouth to protest, but I held up a hand to silence her. "I know, I know, everything has to be more secret than the files at MI5. As I said earlier, I have a number of friends in the police, and one of them, Mandy Hiscoe, is a detective sergeant and she's on maternity leave—"

"Hiscoe? She is not on leave. She was alongside that idiot Quinn last night."

"My mistake. She should be on maternity leave. I'll have a quiet word in her ear and see what I can learn about the caller's identity. I believe this comes down to hacking, and with all due respect to you, Sebastian, the law is much better prepared to investigate and handle such things."

"Can you crack it?" Anita demanded.

"Alone? Probably not. Working alongside my police contacts, I think I might be able to. Why?"

"How much do you charge?"

"Well, Valerie—"

"Never mind Valerie. How much?"

Normally it was forty pounds an hour – and I'd increased it since The Incident and the consequent reduction in our income – but this woman was worth quite a lot of money, so I hyped the charges a bit more. "Fifty pounds an hour plus out of pocket expenses."

"Get some answers, send me an itemised bill and I guarantee you will be paid."

Chapter Six

"I have to say, Chrissy, I've never seen you come on that strong with anyone except Dennis."

"Dennis deserves it, or at least, he used to. So did Anita."

We were back in her Ford, winding our way back down the hill towards town, and I was a mixture of emotions. Happy to take on a contract that might pay me well, but concerned that I could just be biting off a nibble more than I could safely swallow without choking.

Paddy Quinn, the SIO, and I shared a level of mutual distrust. My success in the Graveyard Poisoner inquiry, assisted by Quinn's 2IC, Detective Sergeant Mandy Hiscoe, didn't help. I got to the answer while he was faffing about trying to pin it on someone else. The same thing happened with the Wool Fair, when Mandy and I confronted the real perpetrator while Quinn was interrogating an innocent young man. True he had mellowed a little in the light of The Incident, but I knew it wouldn't last forever, and poking my nose into the murder of Fay Selkirk might just mark the turning point.

I changed the subject as Val dropped into second gear for a steeper stretch of road. "What is it about these novel plots that need to be kept under such close wraps?"

"Other writers stealing the idea," Val replied, concentrating on the twists and turns in the road. "You can't copyright ideas, you see. If two writers turn out similar work, but not the same, it's tough, but it's not illegal unless one can demonstrate that the other stole the idea, and in Anita's case that would be near on impossible. She's always been that way. You heard Seb say that he doesn't read her books. Well, other than me, no one, absolutely no one gets to see anything of her work until they're complete, fully edited and ready for publication. At that stage it goes out to her ARC team."

"Arc team?"

"Advanced Review Copy team. They read and critique the work. But even they're not allowed to give away any plot details. They comment generally and Anita cherry-picks from the comments for inclusion in the front of the book."

"Will she change the plot?"

"She may very well do so."

The road levelled out and before long we joined the town centre bypass.

"Where do you go from here?" Val asked.

"Home. I need to relieve Mrs McQuarrie. And while I'm looking after Dennis, I'll get a quick word with Mandy on the phone, and see where it takes us. Don't worry, Val. I'll clear your name."

It was just gone half past twelve when Val dropped me off. She was in a hurry, so didn't come in, and we parted company at the end of the drive, and I stepped in through the side door to find Hazel helping Dennis get through lunch; a hamburger which she was breaking down into small, manageable pieces and feeding them one by one into his ever-open mouth.

"You don't have to do that, Hazel. He's perfectly capable of picking up small pieces and feeding himself."

She gave Dennis an amused scowl. "You're taking the mickey, aren't you?"

Dennis did not answer, but his lopsided smile told us both the answer.

After a cup of tea and a chat, Hazel left at one o'clock, and once I had cleaned Dennis up, I wheeled him out into the back garden, and dragged my sun lounger closer to his wheelchair. I went indoors to make myself a cheese and salad sandwich, pick up a soft drink, refilled Dennis's cup with lemonade, and when I came outside again, Cappy the Cat had beat me to the sun lounger, the little tyke. He was making himself comfortable when I shooed him off. He wasn't any too happy about that. What is it about cats? I read somewhere that when you have a dog, you're the owner, but when you have a cat, you're the servant. Cappy the Cat certainly worked on that principle.

Because we had a large back garden, a conservatory and a garage, it was almost impossible to hear the front doorbell, so many moons back Dennis had rigged up a chime on the back wall, right behind where we were ensconced. It played something silly like the Can-Can dance, and true to form, it rang just as I finished my sandwich, and I prepared to settle down for some serious me time, aka sleep. Well, what else did I have to do? Anita Stocker was paying me, but despite my assurances to Val, I didn't yet have enough information to approach Mandy or DI Quinn. I also hadn't told Val, but I needed to speak to her husband, and that was the position until I had a clearer idea of what I wanted, and right now, I didn't know what I wanted. Correction. I did. I wanted some sleep, so for the next half hour or so, it was time for an early afternoon siesta.

And someone had the cheek to ring the rotten doorbell.

As I made my way through the house I ran through a mental list of who it might be. Fred and Barbara Timmins were both out at work, Hazel McQuarrie had just gone home, Naomi had to pick Bethany up from pre-school where she attended Monday, Wednesday, and Friday, so it was too early for her, the postman was long gone, and we weren't expecting deliveries of any description, so who…

I opened the door to a vision of male perfection. Much like Sebastian Stocker, only giving out a more charming, less self-centred aura. About six feet tall, looking trim and fit in a pair of brand name denims, Nike trainers, and a short sleeved shirt which showed off his biceps, a carefully cultured and thin, trimmed beard followed the track of a square jawline, while sparkling blue eyes and a pleasant smile playing around kissable lips captured my attention.

"Mrs Capper?"

With thoughts of Ossie Travis and particularly

Sebastian Stocker in mind, I told myself that appearances could be deceptive, and I didn't much care how good looking he was. "That depends on what you're selling."

"I'm not selling anything, but I would like to talk to you. Or more precisely, I'd like to talk to your husband."

"So before I tell you that that is not possible would you like to tell me what you want with him?"

"Impossible? Why?"

"I'm asking the questions. Who are you anyway?"

He dipped his fingers into his shirt pocket and came out with a business card. "Nathan Evanson. I'm a private investigator. Most people call me Nate." He let me see the card, then tucked it back in his pocket.

"I'm a private investigator too. But you still haven't told me what you want with Dennis."

"It's complicated, Mrs Capper. I'd really rather discuss it with him."

"You can talk to him until you're blue in the face, but you won't get any answers, well, none that you can decipher. Who sent you?"

"The police."

As well as hiking my sense of intrigue, it also heightened my suspicions. "A specific officer?"

"Detective Inspector Quinn."

"And he sent you here?"

"He did. Mrs Capper—"

"As and when you tell me what it is you want, I'll consider your request, but until then, why don't you get into your car and disappear? Dennis remembers nothing of The Incident, so he can't tell you anything, and Paddy Quinn should know better. He has all the details anyway and he should have given you the information you want assuming you're not trying to breach confidentiality."

He appeared genuinely puzzled. "Pardon me? The Incident?"

Frustration was beginning to get the better of me. "Who are you working for? And don't tell me the police. They don't employ private eyes and anyway Paddy Quinn hates them as a breed. I know. I speak from experience."

"I'm acting on behalf of WDIG, the Woollen District Insurance Group, and—"

I cut him off again, and by now I was close to snapping. "What? You think Dennis is scamming them for his income protection?" My blood boiling, I stood back. "Come in here. And close the door behind you." My anger increasing with every step, I marched along the hall, through the kitchen and conservatory, and out into the back garden where Dennis was nodding off in his wheelchair. "There you are, Mr private eye. My husband with both legs and his head broken and still heavily bandaged, and if you check the drive, you'll see that the Fiat Diablo is wheelchair accessible, and his power wheelchair is in the garage if you'd like to see that too."

He moved round me, lips pursed and looked Dennis up and down. Then he faced me. "We're at cross purposes here, Mrs Capper. I'm not here to question your husband's disabilities. I didn't even know WDIG were paying out on his income protection policy. I needed to speak to him about another matter entirely, and although I'd be willing to hear what happened to Dennis, I can't understand why DI Quinn sent me here."

"Oh." Having jumped to the understandable but wrong conclusion, something I tended to be quite skilled at, there wasn't much else I could think to say. I made a quick check on Dennis, who was still out of it, and then suggested, "Grab yourself a chair, and maybe I can help you." I waved him to our garden table and the four chairs around it. "Would you like some tea or coffee?"

"Thank you. Coffee would be great."

I returned to the kitchen to make coffee, Cappy the Cat followed me to see if I was about to feed him, but I wasn't, so he disappeared again, and he would probably check on our visitor. He wouldn't stay long. If Mr Evanson didn't feed him, he would be gone in a minute. And sure enough, by the time I got back to the garden, passed a beaker to him, and settled down with one for myself, our picky pussycat had disappeared.

Wearing the same, short skirt I'd put on for Val, I kept my knees closed. The table top was glass, and I was conscious that no matter how attractive the man opposite, the only time Christine Capper's smalls were on show was when they hung on a washing line.

"So," he began, "would you like to tell me what happened to Dennis?"

I gave him chapter and verse on The Incident, and the distant manner in which my investigation into electoral blackmail had precipitated it, the outcome for the perpetrators and the much sadder outcome for me and my husband.

Through the ten, fifteen minute monologue, he barely interrupted and showed no trace of emotion, but when I was through, he apologised.

"Now I understand your reaction at the door, and I am sorry, but I knew nothing about this. Like you, I'm self-employed, and WDIG never said anything. They wouldn't, would they? Mind you, it wasn't them who told me to contact Dennis. They pointed me to DI Quinn and he sent me here."

"I told you. Paddy doesn't like private eyes. He's like it with me all the time. That aside you've wasted your time, Nathan—"

"Nate. Please."

"I'll stick to Nathan if you don't mind, but I'm Chrissy. I'm sorry you've had a wasted journey, unless it's something I can help with." I glanced at the clock. "But you'll have to make it sharp. My daughter-in-law will be here soon, and I have other business I need to attend to."

"Frankly, Chrissy, I wanted to question your husband on something that happened, oh, ten years ago, and it was nothing to do with him really, but he did make a statement apparently. DI Quinn isn't interested because the incident is so long ago, but events over the last twenty-four hours have forced WDIG to rethink the matter, and they've asked me to look into it."

"Events? What events?"

"A young woman murdered in Hattersley Woods yesterday, and a local woman taken in for questioning last night. The witness-stroke-suspect's husband was killed in an accident at his workshop about ten years ago, and WDIG paid out a fortune. Although it's pretty remote, that kind of link is sometimes worth looking into. Your husband knew the man."

The bells, beeps and whistles had begun rattling in my head the moment he mentioned a local woman taken in for questioning. "Bill Duckett?"

For the first time since he rang the doorbell, his eyebrows shot up. "Good god. How did you know?"

I heard the side door open, announcing Naomi's arrival. "Long story, and I'm sorry, but I don't have time to tell it. I told you, I have other business I need to attend to on behalf of Bill Duckett's wife, er, widow. I have an appointment to make and I need to change."

An insouciant smile spread across his face. "Change? Whatever for? You look fantastic."

Whether it was simply flattery or he was several pennies short of the full pound, I don't know, but he certainly gave my ego a much-needed boost.

As I rose, expecting Naomi and Bethany, he suggested, "Let me run you to your appointment, Chrissy. Maybe we can grab a late lunch after. It sounds like we have a lot to talk about. I'll bring you back here when we're through, and I promise I won't run out of petrol on a lonely country road."

"Oh yes? Making assignations while Dennis is laid up, are you, Chrissy?"

It was Naomi announcing her arrival. As I stood up to greet her, a tiny blur rocketed across the decking and leapt into my arms, shouting, "Nanna."

"Assignations, Naomi? Chance would be a fine

thing. Nathan, may I introduce my daughter in-law. Naomi, this is Nathan Evanson, a fellow private eye."

He stood and shook hands with her. "A couple of beautiful ladies from a beautiful family. I envy both your husbands."

I set Bethany down. "You wouldn't be quite so envious if someone had to change your incontinence pants three times a day. Can I leave you with Naomi for a few minutes? Just while I get changed and then I'll gladly accept your offer of a lift."

"Of course."

Chapter Seven

Truth was, I had no appointment. For where we were going, I didn't need one, but I did need to hear what Nathan had to say about Bill Duckett's death, and if he hadn't offered me a lift, I would have asked him to meet me in town later so we could exchange stories. I didn't want Naomi listening in (she would report back to Simon, my son, currently ranked Acting Detective Constable with the Haxford police) and I didn't want to take the chance of Dennis overhearing us and perhaps getting agitated about it.

My suspicions were aroused the moment Val told me that Duckett died when his hydraulic car lift gave way and crushed him, and there was nothing suspicious about it. It was rare that I listened to Dennis – when he could talk, that is – but I was certain he once said those lifts had a failsafe device that prevented them falling on whoever was working beneath them.

Dennis was in no condition to confirm or deny, but Val told me that Tony also knew Bill Duckett and he was suspicious of the death. In that case Tony could tell me, and Nathan Evanson could listen in.

With Nathan's words, 'you look fantastic'

ringing in my ears, I chose my outfit carefully. It wasn't often I got compliments from younger men (note younger, not young) and I did not go out of my way to encourage them but with Haxford Fixers and the mill in general at the forefront of my thinking, I would not get into Nathan's car while dressed in a short skirt. Tongues wagged in Haxford. In fact, I suspect it held the world record for the speed of gossip. Facebook, Twitter, Whatsapp, social media in general, stand aside, all of you, and let Haxford show you how to spread the word quickly and inaccurately. If I climbed into Nathan's car wearing a risky, short skirt and a thin (easily removed) blouse, by the time we were through talking to Tony Wharrier, the world would be persuaded that Nathan and I were popping out for a quickie in Hattersley Woods.

I swilled my face and arms in cold water to wash away the sweat and grim of a hot morning, and applied a couple of dabs of Jimmy Choo's Amber Kiss which Dennis bought for me in Playa de Las Américas. He wasn't actually aware that he'd bought it until the credit card bill came through a month later and he almost had a stroke at the price. I told him it was a bargain, but at £150 a bottle, he was left trying to calculate the cost per sniff. Once suitably perfumed, I put on a pair of jeans and my favourite Blondie T-shirt and joined Nathan and my daughter-in-law on the rear decking.

Nathan was positively astonished. "Wow. Blondie. Any fan of Debbie Harry gets my vote."

"My era, thank you," I said with a shy smile.

"I'm a bit younger, but I love that woman's, er,

energy."

For a terrible moment, I thought he was going to say something more physical and personal about her.

My daughter-in-law guffawed. "Why don't you oldies get about your business, and leave us young 'uns to look after Grandad?"

"You're sure you'll be all right with him, Naomi." I checked my watch. "It's coming up to two. We should be back for four."

"Don't you mean you will be back for four as long as Nate doesn't run out of petrol on a lonely country road?" She laughed again and Nathan joined in. I just blushed. "It's no problem, Chrissy. Now get going."

Two minutes later, convinced that half the street would be peering through their nets, I settled into the comfortable passenger seat of Nathan's VW, he started the engine, reversed into our drive, and drove out, turning to the right for Moor Road.

"Where are we going, Chrissy?"

"My husband's workshop, Haxford Mill. You know it?"

"No. I'm from Bradford. I'm staying at the Haxford Arms but I don't know the town well."

"Isn't that a little extravagant?" I asked. "You know. Staying at a hotel? I mean Bradford's less than twenty miles, isn't it?"

"I can't be bothered with the journey and anyway, I prefer to be on the doorstep when I'm on a case. You never know what might turn up during the night."

"Oh." I let the matter go. "Well, to get to

Haxford Mill, head for town and when you get to the bypass, turn right for Sheffield Road. I'll direct you from there. It's not far."

I spent a moment familiarising myself with the car's interior, found the window switch, and let it down a couple of inches. Nathan promptly sent it back up again. "Aircon," he explained, braking at the end of the street where it joined Moor Road. He flipped a switch on the dashboard. "You'll find it cooler if you leave the window closed." I pursed my lips and murmured my acquiescence, and as he joined the light traffic heading into town, he said, "So tell me about Christine Capper."

"Nothing much to tell, really, and if you were a Haxforder, you'd know it all. I'm just past my half-century, and Dennis and I have been together for thirty years, and we have two children, Simon, who's a police officer – that was his wife, you met, Naomi – and Ingrid who lives in Scarborough and is an entertainer. I used to be a police officer, and these days I'm well-known locally as a vlogger, blogger, private investigator, and I have a fifteen minute slot every Tuesday on Radio Haxford as the agony aunt. That's it. You now know all about Christine Capper. Your turn."

"Same story but different."

He slowed down for the mini island where Moor Road joined the southern town centre bypass, and I directed him to the right. While he was busy manoeuvring with the increasing traffic, I tried to work out how our stories could be the same and yet different.

A couple of minutes later, when we turned onto

Sheffield Road, he went on with his tale.

"I'm forty-five years old and divorced. I'm an ex-redcap. I was a non-com, and when I came out of the military police I applied for the civvy cops, but I wanted CID. I don't have a degree, so they would only take me in uniform and let me work my way up. I told them where to go, and did a bit of security work until I could get my private eye's ticket, and then set myself up. I was lucky. I have an old pal who works for WDIG, and he wangled me in as an investigative consultant, and the rest is history. I'm not bragging, Christine, but I have a good track record with them."

"Exposing the scammers, clawing back money which has been falsely claimed?"

"You've got it. Looking at your husband, it's obvious why you jumped to that conclusion when I first knocked on your door, and I'm sorry." He paused for a moment while I directed him along Haxford Mill Road. As we passed through the outer walls of the mill grounds, he spoke up again. "You haven't told me who we're going to see and why."

"All will become clear in a few minutes." I pointed to the left hand side of the vast building, along the track of the wall which separated the mill from the canal beyond. "Haxford Fixers are just along there. You'll see their van, and if you park somewhere alongside it, we'll get down to brass tacks."

He left his car in the shade of Dennis's tow truck, a huge, ungainly thing, capable of pulling everything from cars to medium-sized vans. We climbed out into the searing heat, and ambled into the workshop.

Aside from Dennis's absence nothing had changed. In the far corner, Lester Grimes, the electrical appliance specialist, sat at his bench, working on a vacuum cleaner, its innards disgorged while he fiddled with it, a Seat Toledo stood over the maintenance pit, its hood raised and Greg Vetch was bent over the engine. From the bodywork shop next door, I could hear the sounds of someone tinkering: Tony Wharrier.

Lester was the first to spot us. He turned a toothless grin on us, and said, "Hey up, Chrissy. Fed up of changing Cappy's nappies? Decided you wanted to see some real men hard at it? And who's this with you?"

"Nathan Evanson, Lester. Nathan, can I introduce you to Dennis's business partner, Lester Grimes."

Nathan smiled. "Pleased to meet you, Lester."

"Most folk call me Grimy, but bear this in mind, fella, I have first refusal on Christine when she is ready for dropping—"

"Yes. Thank you, Lester. Give Tony a shout, will you?"

During the exchange, Greg emerged from under the Seat. About the same age as Dennis, he was much shorter, more rotund, and he'd been called in to replace my husband as the mechanical wizard.

"Hello, Christine. How's Dennis?"

"No change, Greg. Nathan, this is Greg Vetch. He was drafted in to take over from Dennis after The Incident."

"I won't shake hands, Nathan. You look too

clean for that, but I'm pleased to meet you."

"The feeling's mutual, Greg."

Lester came back from the body shop. "Geronimo's here."

I went through the introductions again, explaining Tony Wharrier's nickname, and this time Nathan and Tony shook hands, before my husband's senior partner, brought us to business.

"What can I do for you, Christine?"

"Bill Duckett."

Tony's eyes wandered around the workshop as he racked his memory, and at the same time Greg spoke up. "Willie Duckett? He's been dead a good ten years."

Now I perked up. "You knew him, too, Greg?"

"He worked at Addison's when I were an apprentice. We all knew him, didn't we Geronimo? Me, your Dennis and Geronimo here."

Tony nodded. "What about him, Christine?"

I handed over to Nathan.

"I represent the insurance company which paid out on his death, Tony, and certain circumstances have come to light over the last twenty-four hours which calls into question the cause of his death. At the same time, I think Christine has some queries on the same subject."

"A related matter, as it happens, Tony," I said, "and I can't really tell you anything, but I was with Val this morning, and she told me that you were suspicious of Billy's death all those years ago. I'm sure Dennis felt the same way."

"You're right. He did. But, listen, this place is hardly right for this kind of discussion. What say we moved to the Snacky? Greg, you and Lester can hold the fort for half an hour, can't you?"

"No problem, Geronimo," Lester agreed.

Sandra's Snacky was the only eatery in the mill and it was on the third, uppermost floor. Owned and run by Sandra Limpkin, a woman a few years younger than me, it catered mainly for the employees of the numerous businesses based in the building, and the few customers who had to wait for whatever they had called there for. Customers like Dennis's who maybe left their car for minor repair work and made their way to the Snacky to wait for the job completing. I often wondered how many had turned up expecting to wait half an hour and ended up taking breakfast, lunch, and afternoon tea in the Snacky. My husband was an excellent auto engineer, but notoriously picky. If you complained of a tricky brake, he'd strip every assembly on every wheel, and if you came in expecting a bill of, say, twenty pounds, you probably wouldn't get much change out of eighty.

The partners at Haxford Fixers were amongst Sandra's oldest and most loyal customers, and when we arrived, she gave me a cheery smile and in a voice loud enough to be heard in Huddersfield, asked after Dennis. I'd known her many years and she was what I termed WYSIWYG: what you see is what you get. Her motto amounted to, call a spade a ******* (*insert Anglo-Saxon term of preference*) shovel and be done with it.

I gave her the appropriate assurances regarding Dennis, and the three of us sat at a table.

Hands clasped around his beaker, Tony led with

a question. "So what did you want to know, Christine? I mean, as Greg said, Billy's been dead for all of ten years."

"I know. I spent an hour with his widow this morning."

The announcement caused Nathan some surprise, but brought a broad smile to Tony's features.

"Janet? Lovely woman. How is she?"

"Still lovely unfortunately, and very wealthy."

"Was that the reason Val wanted you to ring?"

"I'm bound by client confidentiality, Tony, and I can't discuss it with anyone, but yes, that's why Val rang. If you want to know any more, you'll have to speak to her. You were saying about Janet."

"Wealthy, you said, and so she should be. He was insured to the hilt, you know." He laid an eye on Nathan. "But you'd know that already, wouldn't you? They had this farm up on the moors. That was worth more than a shilling or two. Last I heard, after he died, she sold up and shipped out to Portugal or somewhere."

"Well, you heard wrong. She has an apartment in southern Spain but she still lives at Hilly Farm. And she told me all about it. He was insured for a hefty sum—"

"One hundred thousand pounds," I interrupted, "and the mortgage on the farm was insured, too, and—"

"What mortgage?"

Tony's interruption stopped me, while Nathan gawped. "What?"

"What mortgage?"

"The mortgage on the farm."

Tony sorted. "My eye and new bolt-on wings. Billy lived on that farm all his life. It was his dad's afore him."

"It was probably remortgaged, Tony," Nathan explained.

"For all the modernisation work, I should imagine," I said. "It's certainly been brought well up to date. Either way it was paid off when her husband said goodbye to this earth. Now listen, Tony, I'm not so much interested in—"

The last thing he did was listen. He talked right over me. "I could never understand why a good-looking lass like that married an old duffer like Billy."

"Val married you," I protested. "Someone has to take pity on you men."

"Yeah, but she's Valerie, isn't she? Janet is, you know, like... you know... Well, she's Janet." His voice sounded as dreamy as mine when my imagination wandered off to desert islands with Bloomy and Deppy.

This was a side of Tony Wharrier I had never seen, and it came as something of a surprise. I felt duty bound to give him a gentle ticking off. "Tony, have you thought how comfortable you'll be sleeping in the garage for the next three weeks if Val hears you saying something like that?"

His frown told me that he still hadn't realised how close he would come to a periorbital haematoma... that's a black eye to me and you. It was one of those trivial facts I picked up on an episode of *The Chase* a few nights back.

I took another swallow of tea. "I'm not interested

in miss gorgeous, nineteen forty-seven. Both I and Nathan are interested in how Mr Duckett came to die by accident. You'll have to bear with me on this, but if I remember what Dennis told me, it can't have happened the way it's supposed to have. At least, I think that's what Dennis said."

Nathan, obviously feeling a little left out, chose to contribute. "I've read the reports, and they say that Mr Duckett was working under the vehicle raised on his auto lift, and the assembly failed. The car came down on top of him and crushed him to death. You're an auto technician, Tony, you know as well as I do that those auto lifts are fitted with a safety cut-out. The ramp would only come so far down and it would stop long before it could crush him."

Without being aware of it, Nathan had confirmed my suspicion. For the accident to happen the way it was described was – according to Dennis and now Nathan – impossible.

Tony's face became more serious. "The police insisted it was an accident. Dennis didn't believe that and when he explained it to me, I was suspicious too, so we told that friend of yours, Paddy Quinn, but he wouldn't have it. Told us to get lost."

"Paddy Quinn might have mellowed a little since The Incident, but he's no friend of mine and never has been."

It was as if I hadn't said anything. Tony went on, his features becoming grim. "Y'see, Christine, we knew Billy. Me and Dennis, and Greg Vetch. We all knew him from Addison's." He went on, speaking mainly to Nathan. "I'm a bodywork specialist, but Dennis, Christine's husband, is a mechanical genius. That's not just flattery. It's a fact, and Christine will back me up on it. Well, Bill Duckett taught him. He was a good deal older than us, was Bill, and he taught Dennis and Greg everything they know about engines. Huge man, you know, Bill." Tony flexed his muscles (buried beneath his overalls) and then placed his hand on his belly and lifted them away a few inches.

I recalled the photograph I'd seen on Janet/Anita's mantelpiece: the one she'd looked at when deciding whether to talk to Val and me. "You mean fat?" I asked.

"Fattish, but he was very strong. Packed quite a punch so we were led to believe."

"And a paunch," Nathan commented with a wry grin. "Sorry, Tony. Do go on."

Tony gave him a strange look, and then went on. "Anyway, he left Addison's while we were still serving our apprenticeships, and set himself up in business. I tell you, there was no finer mechanic, and he was no fool. His was a two post auto lift, and they have locks fitted. You set the lock and if the lift fails for any reason, it won't come down any further than those locks. And, by the way, it wasn't hydraulic. It was electric. And like I say, we knew Billy. He wouldn't be working under a car without setting the locks."

"Was he alone in the place?" Nathan asked.

"So they say. That lad of theirs, Sebastian, toffee nosed little so and so, he is. Spends most of his time looking in a mirror making sure his hair's perfect.

And what a name. Whoever heard of a boy from Haxford called Sebastian?"

At this point, I felt obliged to cut in. "There's nothing wrong with Sebastian as a given name, Tony. Dennis and I thought of Lucas for Simon before he was born."

"I remember him telling me. Until he pointed out that it'd be shortened to Lew Capper and that would make him sound like a lavatory lid. Anyway, getting back to Seb Duckett, he used to do odd days with his dad, but he was never really into mechanicking. I told you. He's a snobby little worm with an 'I do love me' attitude. And on that day he was out with some young woman somewhere. Probably in Hattersley Woods doing what comes naturally, because his sort usually are. And Janet was up at the farm according to the tale. That only made it all the more puzzling. I'm telling you, Chrissy, Nathan, Billy wasn't daft. On his own, working under the lift, no way would he forget to set the locks." Tony risked a glance at his watch. "Still, it's ten years ago now, isn't it, and who cares? Janet certainly doesn't, does she? All that money, a place in Spain. She's creaming it, isn't she? Loaded since Billy clocked out."

"There are other things in life besides money, Tony," I told him as I finished off the tea. "You say you can't understand why she married him?"

"Billy was considerably older than her."

"Really? Was there much of an age difference? Only the way she tells it, they were about the same age." It occurred to me as I posed the question that Anita had never discussed her and her husband's relative ages.

"Nothing near," Tony told me. "At the time of his death, she was in her forties, but Billy was turned sixty."

Chapter Eight

Never one for drinking during the day, and with Dennis to consider, a late pub lunch was not an option, but Bellaby's Garden Centre stood between Haxford Mill and the town centre, and when Nathan insisted he needed something to eat, I suggested the cafeteria there.

Once upon a time it had been a family business, but it was taken over by one of the national supermarkets about twenty years back, and they sold it off to another large, national concern five years ago. It had the advantage that although one or two of the staff knew me from my vlog and blog, I was not on speaking terms with any of them, which in turn meant Nathan and I could talk in something approaching privacy and without interruptions from well-wishers asking after Dennis.

The place was not too busy. Well, it wouldn't be in the middle of a Wednesday afternoon when most people were at work. After ordering at the counter – a cold meat and cheese salad for me, quiche for him – we managed to find a table in a quiet corner, and as we sat down away from other customers, it occurred to me that to anyone taking particular notice, we might be lovers on a clandestine meeting.

Nathan would be ideal for the role. I'd known

him for less than two hours, but I assessed him as easy-going, charming, fun to be with (look at the way he laughed when Naomi echoed his comment about him running out of petrol on a lonely country lane), physically fit and good looking. The latter wasn't just me either. I noticed the way the young woman behind the counter ran an appreciative eye over him.

I wasn't stupid enough or naïve enough to assume that he was attracted to me. His brief comments at home were, I guessed, no more than saucy flattery, designed to raise a smile, and I'm no different to any other woman coming into her middle years. It tickled my fancy when someone told me how good looking I was, even if I didn't really believe it.

We kept the conversation neutral while eating. I told him a little bit more about me and my down-to-earth, working-class background (is there such a background these days?) and I learned a little more about him, how he had grown up in a simple household, his father a lorry driver, his mother a picker and packer in a mail-order warehouse, and how, after leaving school with a couple of top grade GCSE passes, he held a series of different jobs before joining the army at the age of eighteen, and eventually became a military policeman. He made the rank of sergeant by the time he gave it up twenty years later, and after turning down the police, he took the same private investigator's course as I did.

That final item scored him several more points in my estimation. I keep saying, and it's spelled out in bold letters on my blog bio, that I was the only properly trained and qualified private investigator in Haxford, but now and then I would meet people calling themselves private eyes who were no more than debt collectors trying to hype their reputation.

We were onto our second cup of tea when the conversation turned to business, and it was Nathan who led.

"Okay, so we're both interested in the death of Bill Duckett. I'm guessing you understand, but I think I know what prompted WDIG's interest."

"The murder of Fay Selkirk last night?"

"In a roundabout way, yes. Some of our people are well in with the police, and when they took Janet Duckett in for questioning, the alerts started to flash. Suppose you tell me how you got involved."

So I told him of Val's visit and the spark that ignited the inquiry, and followed up with my visit to Hilly Farm and the interchange with Janet.

"She prefers to be known as Anita Stocker, the name she writes her books under. The moment Val told me about Bill Duckett's death, I became suspicious, because I was so sure Dennis had told me about the safety devices on that kind of machinery. All of which you know from our discussion with Tony. I didn't broach Bill's death with Anita, but she insists she had nothing to do with Fay Selkirk's murder, and she's adamant that someone read the first chapter of this new book. I could be completely wrong about her, Nathan, but I believe her. You obviously don't."

"That's not what I'm saying, Chrissy. But there are some curious anomalies, and you've just added to them. Did you say that in Utter Carnage, the murder takes place on page ten?"

Did I? It was only a few moments ago and I couldn't remember. "I'm not sure I said anything of the kind, but you're right."

Nathan leaned forward, arms resting on the table, reached across, took my left, and studied my wedding, engagement, and eternity rings. "Why are all the best looking women already married?"

I laughed and retracted my hand. Wagging a disapproving finger at him, I said, "You're doing my confidence a power of good, but I'm an old-fashioned, one man woman. I'm also a clever private eye so stop trying to distract me. Now what's this about page ten?"

"Have you ever read any of Anita Stocker works?"

"About three or four hundred words of Utter Carnage. That was enough."

"Yeah, I suppose they are a bit graphic. Her first novel was entitled, simply, *Crushed*, and it was all about a motor mechanic who was crushed under his auto lift, and when the police investigate, they learn that the safety locks were not set. Does that tale sound familiar?"

"Yes. I'm sure someone said her first book was based on Bill's death. In fact, come to think, I believe it was Anita herself who told me."

Nathan appeared satisfied with my answer. "I read the whole book and as the story progresses, it becomes apparent that the victim didn't die by accident. He was murdered. Janet, Anita if you prefer, has turned out thirty or forty books, and in most cases, the first murder takes place on page ten."

I buried the slight surprise. "You sound like a dedicated fan of her work."

"I'm afraid not. I enjoy a good whodunit, but frankly I'd rather have a comedy. I don't like all that blood and guts gore."

"But you think there was something more to Bill Duckett's death, don't you? You think he was murdered in exactly the same way the victim died in her first book, and… What? You think she did it?" I didn't wait for Nathan to answer. "You're working for the insurance company, so are they saying that the pay-out would be invalid if it could be proven that Bill was murdered?"

He frowned and spent a moment or two in silence, obviously thinking about the proposition. When he eventually replied, he was hazy. "There's no doubt that Bill Duckett died before *Crushed* was published, but who's to say that the original manuscript wasn't written before his death? Think about it, Chrissy. He died in February, ten years ago. *Crushed* was published in July, but how do we know that the original manuscript wasn't written in, say, January? So, would it affect the insurance claim? No… Unless Anita Stocker, Janet Duckett, call her what you will, committed the crime as an act of bizarre research. Since she was the beneficiary, the company would be in a position to reclaim the £180,000 they paid out on both his life assurance and the mortgage protection insurance."

"And, to boot, they'd send Anita to prison for an awful long time. And I wouldn't argue with that, but I think it will be hell's teeth of a job to prove."

He gave me a not quite so modest smile. "Why do you think WDIG have called me in?"

The fake hubris – I was sure it was not meant to be taken seriously – caused me to laugh. "I love your self-confidence."

"Trust me, Chrissy, there's a lot more about me to love than my confidence."

I had to wonder for the moment whether it was a double entendre, but I let it pass. "I have to confess, when I read this excerpt from Utter Carnage, and compared it to the report in last night's Haxford Recorder, the first thing that occurred to me was that Anita had committed the murder. I have contacts in the police, but I haven't spoken to them yet. I was going to when you rang the doorbell."

"That's me. Always turn up in exactly the wrong moment."

I laughed again. Dennis excepted, I had never felt so comfortable in the company of a man.

Nathan leaned forward again. "Listen, Chrissy, we both have a vested interest in this matter. What say we combine our investigations?"

"It sounds like a good idea." I was lying. It was an idea with all the attraction of an industrial sized electromagnet... whatever one of those is. "But Anita is the one paying me to demonstrate that she has nothing to do with Fay Selkirk. If she really is the killer and you can prove it, and moreover, if you prove that she murdered her husband, I won't get paid."

A frown etched itself across his clear brow. "I can see how that would be a problem to you, especially with Dennis the way he is. Let me ask, how much do you charge?"

"It used to be twenty an hour, but I've had to increase my charges since… since Dennis. I'm now charging anything between thirty and fifty an hour depending on the client's circumstances."

His eyebrows shot up. "You're working for peanuts."

I sighed. "I don't live in the big city, Nathan. This is Haxford. Even with my higher profile since the ballot box business, people aren't exactly climbing over one another to get to my door. And I'm very choosy about the cases I take on. I don't get involved in criminal matters… well, not intentionally. It seems to happen that way, but I don't set out to hunt down criminals. So I keep my prices low. And, before The Incident, it was just a part time job. I'd hate to think that Dennis and I were going to have to become dependent on it, but his income protection runs out after a year, and if he doesn't improve by then…"

I trailed off, not wanting to state the obvious, and at the same time, I almost squirmed in my seat. Why was I suddenly embarrassed at spelling out my charges? I had never apologised for them in the past.

"Obviously, I charge out-of-pocket expenses too," I concluded. "Let me ask you the same question. If you don't mind, that is. How much do you charge?"

He shrugged. "It depends on the job. Taking a statement for divorce, eighty-five pounds an hour plus expenses. The more complex the case, the more I charge, all the way up to a maximum of a hundred and forty pounds an hour. And where WDIG is concerned, I also pick up one percent of any monies I can recoup. So, for example, if I can prove that Janet Duckett murdered her husband, and they get back the entire hundred and eighty grand – a longshot, I'll grant you – I'll collect a bonus of eighteen hundred quid."

It occurred to me just how cheap I really was working, and I almost fainted.

Nathan wasn't yet finished. "Let me make you an offer. I don't say that this is the case, but if we can demonstrate that Janet Duckett really did murder her husband, I will pay whatever fees are due to you, the money she should have paid you, plus a cut of whatever bonus I pick up. Say ten percent. How does that sound?"

Before The Incident, Dennis would have worked such as calculation out in a matter of seconds. It took me slightly longer, but if that turned out to be the case, not only would I pick up my hourly charges, say six hundred pounds, but Nathan would top it up with another hundred and eighty. That was assuming we cracked the case in a matter of a few days.

"Us crumbling old beggars can't be choosers," I said. "I accept."

He beamed. "Good. Great. Just what I like to hear." The frown returned. "All except one thing."

"Which is?"

"Why do you run yourself down so much? Take it from me, Chrissy, you're a good-looking woman, and you shouldn't belittle yourself like that."

"Actually, I meant it as a joke. I know I'm a good-looking woman. I can see every time a look in a mirror." This time he laughed, and while he was chuckling away, I checked the time. "It's quarter to four, Nathan. I have to be getting home. I know Naomi doesn't mind, but she has a husband and a little girl to look after, and I can't ask her to nursemaid Dennis for hours and hours on end."

"Of course. Let's get you back to Bracken Close."

A few minutes later, sat in his car, and on the way home, he asked, "Your police contact. It's not Paddy Quinn, is it?"

"Dear me, no. I worked with Paddy when he was in uniform years ago, and we never really got on. And over the last half year or so, I've beaten him to the perpetrator a couple of times. The way he was with you is the way he is with every private eye, so don't take it personally. No, my contact is Detective Sergeant Amanda Hiscoe. We're old friends, me and Mandy. She's very pregnant and due to go on mat' leave any time now, but according to what I've been told, she sat in on the interrogation of Anita Stocker yesterday, so I'll have a quick word with her over the phone tonight, and if you wish, I can arrange to meet her on neutral ground tomorrow. Terry's Tea Bar in the market hall is where we usually get our heads together, but with Dennis in mind, it'll probably be my place."

"And will she be forthcoming?"

The question brought a smile to my lips and to demonstrate that I could be as fly as him when it came to the occasional double entendre, I said, "She was certainly forthcoming with some man six or seven months back."

He cackled. "She's unmarried?"

"And determined to stay that way," I said with a nod. More seriously, I went on, "She shares information, Nathan, but we have an understanding. I keep her abreast of everything I learn, and if it comes to an arrest, she's the one who deals with it, not me. I don't do heroics."

"Sounds about right to me."

He turned into Bracken Close, drove up to our bungalow and reversed into the drive. "Okay. Ten tomorrow morning? Or is that too early?"

I shrugged. "I never know from one day to another. Some days Dennis can be up for eight. Other days, it can be four in the morning and he'll then go back to bed until noon, but don't worry. I'll make arrangements with Mandy."

"Fine. I'll be on the doorstep at ten tomorrow."

I watched him drive away and as I turned to go into the house I stopped and stared at the place for a long moment. We had been happy here for the last three decades. Now happy was the last word that sprang to mind, and along with others, usually coming to me in my darker moments, that very thought felt so treacherous.

For the umpteenth time in the last month and more, I cursed the animals (it was the only word I could think of when I saw what they did to my husband) who had brought us to this.

Naomi was sat outside at the back skimming through a fashion magazine when I came out through the conservatory. Bethany was asleep on the sun lounger, her arms around Cappy the Cat who didn't even bother to wake up when I appeared. Dennis was noticeable by his absence.

"Nursie's been," Naomi told me. "She changed his dressings and put him back to bed with his legs raised." She checked her watch. "That was about an hour ago. We need to lower his legs, but when I checked, he was asleep and I didn't like to disturb him."

"I'm sorry I've been so long. You're sure you don't mind?"

"Course not. What would I do at home but sit around the back garden reading and keeping an eye on madam?" She waved vaguely at her sleeping daughter. "How did you get on?"

"We made a little progress. Not much, but enough to agree that Nathan and I will work together on this case. I don't want to say any more, Naomi, because we could be miles off base, and I don't want you sending Simon on wild goose chases."

"No problem. And if it gets you out of the house with Nate, go for it. He's very tasty."

I laughed. "He is quite dishy, isn't he?"

"Dishy? Talk about retro. Cast me as Sandy in a new production of Grease. How old are you, Chrissy? He's a babe magnet."

"Is he? Well, I'm sorry but I'm not a babe."

Chapter Nine

Weather-wise, Thursday morning was a replica of Wednesday and while waiting for Dennis to wake up, I prepared the sun lounger for occupation, only to have Cappy the Cat make another attempt to get there before I shooed him off. Having found him in a cosy cuddle with Bethany the previous afternoon, I believed that cat was getting just too comfortable on that lounger. He gave me a familiar, 'I will make you regret that' type glare and hurried off to visit Fred and Barbara next door.

It was curious how he always chose the Timmins's garden and never Hazel McQuarrie's. Or perhaps he just knew that with Hazel he had to do as he was told.

I'd had a bad night. Between attending to Dennis and the various, unconnected and disparate thoughts rushing round my head, I'd had little sleep.

Bill Duckett, Dennis, Fay Selkirk, Dennis, Nathan Evanson, Bill Duckett, Dennis, Janet (Anita Stocker) Duckett, Nathan Evanson, Dennis, Paddy Quinn, Fay Selkirk, Sebastian Duckett, Nathan Evanson, murder, accident, Dennis, on and on and on, my febrile mind flitting, jumping from one focus to another. It was enough to drive me crazy.

And it was Thursday, the day I traditionally

recorded my vlog. I hadn't given it any consideration, I had no topic, no approach, and five weeks on from The Incident, I was sure my viewers would soon be sick of hearing about Dennis and his problems, and talking about the weather was so… so British.

I broached the manner in which Dennis's care was getting to me when speaking to Mandy on the phone the previous night. She asked, and I let the anxiety pour out.

"Respite care," she replied without hesitation. "Think about it, Chrissy. Put Dennis into respite care and get yourself off to Benidorm for a week."

I didn't tell her that I'd already thought of and dismissed the option. "Benidorm? Who with? Not you. So far into your pregnancy, the airline would never let you on the plane. And I can't think of anyone else, and going alone, I might just as well stay here. Besides, I'm not sure we can afford respite care. According to my research, it costs hundreds of pounds a day."

We went on for some time, batting backwards and forwards over different issues, and ultimately when I told her of my inquiries the previous day, she agreed to come out and see me at ten o'clock.

"There'll be another private investigator with us. A man named Nathan Evanson."

She did not sound enthusiastic. "From Bradford. We know him. He gave Paddy some earache yesterday about the death of a mechanic ten years ago and Paddy sent him on a wild goose chase."

"Yes, he did. He sent him to me and told him to ask for Dennis."

Familiar irritation was the response this time. "Oh my god. I'm sorry, Chrissy. You know what Paddy's like, and this Selkirk murder has him hyped up. I'll see you at ten in the morning, and I'll listen to whatever you have to say, but you know the rules. Whatever you know, I need to know."

We left it at that, and after cooking Dennis his meal, then cleaning up after him, I sat him in front of the TV and brought my case notes up to date.

When you train as a private eye, one of the first things they teach you is the necessity of taking notes. It's good practice. Well, I was out of practice. Truth is, I never really got into practice. It was one of my few failings (yes, I remained convinced that I don't have many failings). I tended to commit too much to memory, but as luck would have it, I have an excellent memory.

As if to compensate, when working on a case, I brought my notes up-to-date every evening, and while Dennis watched endless repeats of Top Gear on one of the digital channels (I wasn't sure that he could still understand them) I detailed the day's events in chronological order with rough timings.

An hour after starting, when I read through them, I was startled to find a comment attached to the paragraph detailing Nathan's arrival. *Would I? You bet I would.* The meaning was instantly clear to me, and in many ways, I was certain that meaning was the catalyst for the sleep deprivation.

Discounting Dennis's infirmities, libidinous indulgence did not trouble us often. You read reports of couples in their eighties who still enjoy a healthy, vibrant sex life. We didn't enjoy anything of the kind in our forties, and although it might sound like a reversal of the traditional situation, it was down to Dennis not me. Dominated by an obsession with engines, he had never been demanding in the bedroom department, and although I wouldn't have objected to more action, I was one of those women who needed someone to press the switch. Therefore, our bedroom activities rarely amounted to anything more exciting than reading and sleeping.

In the course of my activities, I'd met any number of handsome men, some of them exuding a raw sensuality. Ossie Travis, a man I encountered during the Haxford Wool Fair case, was one such example. But fanciful daydreams aside, that's as far as it went, and I would never include any such reference in my notes.

Nathan Evanson was no different. Good-looking, charming, laid-back, totally confident, free with the compliments, some of them bordering on the naughty, he was, as Naomi said, a babe magnet (yuk). But as I said to her, I was not a babe. I was fifty-three years of age, a mature, sensible, married woman, stress 'married'.

The inclusion of this appalling comment, *'Would I? You bet I would'*, was easy to diagnose, but it was telling me something that I didn't really want to hear.

I couldn't recall any fantasy of Nathan and I entwined on the mattress, but there were those lurid dreams involving me and Deppy and Bloomy. This was not a need for gratuitous satisfaction. It was precisely the opposite. An expression on my *dissatisfaction*, of the pressure heaped upon me by our complex circumstances. Respite care, Mandy had suggested, the need to get away from everything for a little while. Those six words in my case notes underlined exactly that need.

But I couldn't do it. How could I leave Dennis in the care of strangers (all right, so even I was a stranger to him, and he'd been in the care of doctors and nurses, all of them strangers to him, for three weeks before he came home) and enjoy myself away from it all? As I thought about it in broader terms, I knew it would not work. Forget Benidorm, if I went over to Scarborough to stay with Ingrid and her boyfriend for a few days, I would do nothing but worry about Dennis.

I had to find a way to reconcile everything, deal with it, cope with it. And it's what we women are supposed to be best at, isn't it? Coping.

And so, I spent a restless night in our king-sized bed, tossing, turning, waking, dozing, until eight o'clock in the morning, when I finally gave up the ghost, and dragged my weary bones into the shower.

Sat outside, taking in the nine a.m. sunshine, savouring my first cup of tea of the day, the whole mess came back to haunt me, and attempts at distraction, concentrating on the murder of Fay Selkirk and the death of Bill Duckett, proved pointless. I kept coming back to myself, my problems, my husband, my absolute mess of a life.

My father was a practical man all his life, and I remembered when I was young, recently settled down with Dennis, and there would be those times when I would visit and complain about a major argument. Dad gave me some simple advice.

"Problems are there to be solved, lass. You don't sort them by running away and coming to me and your mam. You face up to them. Admit you have a problem, work it out, sort it out, and get on with your life."

And ever since that brief conversation, I had stood by that advice. Dennis and I were like any other couple. We had our share of issues, problems, albeit most of them minor, but when they reared their ugly head, I met them head on. There were no long, sulky silences in our house. Well, there were, but it was usually Dennis sulking, and it never took me long to bring him round.

For the past five weeks I had been dealing with the most serious problem we had ever faced. Again, I took Dad's advice and confronted it. To no avail. It wasn't that there was no solution. There were several, all of them equally unsatisfactory. The real issue was the problem itself. It was intractable, immovable, unremitting, refusing to go away, refusing to reconcile, and the only way I would ever resolve it was for Dennis to get better, become again the man I loved, the man I chose to spend my life with. He was making progress, true, but it was slow, snail pace, and the day when he would once again be fully independent seemed as distant as that break in Benidorm.

Thoughts of our favourite resort on the Costa Blanca prompted another idea. If a few days on the coast would do me good, what would it do for Dennis?

I didn't know, and I didn't want to get into long and detailed question and answer sessions with the doctors. Not when there was another source of such information nearby.

Making sure I had my phone in the pocket of my shorts in case Dennis hit the panic button, I made my way through the house, out through the side door, and next door to Hazel McQuarrie's.

"Come on in, Chrissy," she said when she opened the door. "Not often I have visitors, and you'll have to excuse the mess. I keep telling myself it's time to tidy up, but I never seem to get round to it." She limped back into her kitchen, waved me to a seat at the table, and switched the kettle on. "You'll have tea?"

It was a query, but it came across as more of an instruction, and I agreed.

The exterior of her bungalow was smart, well kept, like ours. I knew she employed a local handyman to keep the garden tidy – something else I might have to think about while Dennis was too ill to do the job – and I helped when I could, taking her bins out for weekly collection, and picking up odds and sods of detritus from her path as I did so.

The interior did not reflect the outside's tidiness. There were heaps of cups, saucers, plates, glasses in the sink, half a loaf of bread on the worktop with a knife nearby, and when she opened the fridge to take out a carton of milk, I noticed that it was covered in slime and grime. I made a vow to myself to find a little time, come round and tidy up for her, maybe with Naomi's help.

"So, to what do I owe the honour?" She placed a

chipped beaker in front of me. "Is it Dennis?"

"In a roundabout way, Hazel, yes. I need some advice, and you're the nearest source I could think of." I took a wet of tea and almost grimaced. I masked it with a smile. "You used to be a nurse."

"Oh, aye? Medical matters is it? Want to know when he'll be fit for a bit of the old how's your father?"

For a terrible moment, I thought she must have read my case notes, or seen something in my face. I laughed it off. "Chance would be a fine thing. And that was before The Incident. No, it's a simple enough query, but I'll bet the answer isn't so simple. I'm under pressure, Hazel. I could do with a few days away."

Frown came to her ageing face. "I don't mind helping for the odd hour or two, Chrissy, but I couldn't babysit him for a week."

"You're jumping the gun, love. I'm not asking you to take care of him. I want to know if it would do Dennis any good. You know, get away from here for a week or two. Our Ingrid lives in Scarborough. I'm sure she could fix something up for us."

She thought about it for the moment. "Offhand, and remember, I'm no doctor, I'd say it would do both him and you of power of good, but he's not ready for it yet. His legs need to mend, Chrissy. All right, I know you can take the wheelchair, but right now, he can barely get out of bed and into the chair. Can you imagine what it would be like in a hotel or a caravan? You've never get him up the steps into a caravan for a start off, and you can't always rely on what these hotels say about disabled access. Give him a bit more time, let his bones mend, let the physios do a bit of work on him. A month from now, could see a world of difference, and at that stage, he might just be ready." She reached across the table and took my hand. "I know this is a flaming nightmare for you, but if I know anything about Christine Capper, it's that she's a strong woman, and your old man's just as strong. He'll get there, Chrissy. You both will, and if you need a bit of a break, give me a shout. I'll come and sit with him while you get out there and get rat-legged."

I laughed at the idea. "And who'd take care of him the following morning while I recovered from a hangover? Thanks, Hazel. I'll take it all on board."

Chapter Ten

An alert call from Dennis forced me to abandon the dregs of my tea, and hurry back home to help him out of bed, into the wheelchair, to the commode, and from there to the kitchen, where I settled him down with a bowl of cereal and a cup of tea. As I put them on the tray in front of him, the doorbell rang, and I scurried through to let Nathan in and as I did, I noticed he was carrying a black briefcase. Things were about to step up a gear.

"Morning," I greeted him. "I'm in the middle of seeing to Dennis. If you want to make your way through the conservatory and out into the back garden, I'll make you a brew and join you as soon as I can."

"No rush, Chrissy."

A clatter from the kitchen told me that Dennis had dropped either his cup or the cereal bowl. When I got to him, it was to find the bowl overturned on the black tiles, and a mess of mulched Weetabix spread everywhere. It wasn't the disaster it might have been. Ever since he came home, I'd been feeding him from plastic basins and plates so at least there was no broken crockery.

"Soz," he said in his now-familiar soft voice.

"Don't worry about it. Do you want any more?"

His response was a shake of the head. "Do you want to go outside?"

This time he nodded, and I wheeled him out into the rear garden, settled him by the table where Nathan was studying the antics of Cappy the Cat trying to chase the birds away from the feeder which hung about eight feet above him.

"I'm sorry, Nathan. Slight domestic disaster. Can I leave you with Dennis while I clean up the mess? I promise I won't be long."

"Of course. Stop worrying, Chrissy. I have all the time in the world."

I scuttled back into the kitchen, switched the kettle on for the second time, and while I was waiting for it to boil, I cleaned up the mess on the floor. The noise must have alerted Cappy the Cat to the possibility of food, and even while I was busy mopping it up, he came rushing in and decided to lend me a hand by licking up some of the spilt milk and chomping away at odd morsels of Weetabix. I swear that cat behaved more and more like a dog every day.

The kettle boiled, I made tea for Nathan and myself, and I was about to carry them out when the doorbell rang. Mandy. It had to be. I rushed out into the garden, handed Nathan a beaker of tea, put the second one down for me, rushed back into the kitchen, switched the kettle on for the third time, and then dashed to the front door to let her in.

"It's a madhouse, Mandy. If you want to go straight through to the garden you will find Nathan with Dennis. Park your BTM and I'll bring you some tea."

She gave me a curious look. "You look harassed."

"Something to do with disabled husbands, crazy cats, and everyone turning up at the same time. Go join them and I'll be with you in a minute."

When I finally sat with them, Mandy and Nathan were chatting, comparing notes on the differences of life in the military and civvy police services, and Dennis was listening. I guessed that from the way his eyes were still open. Were he not listening, he would be asleep by now. By the time I sat with them, sweat was breaking out on my forehead, and it wasn't all to do with the hot sun.

"You want to learn to calm down, girl," Mandy said. "You're tearing around like a blue—"

"Yes, thank you, Mandy. I think we all get the picture."

Dennis smiled and aimed a stare at me. "A looker."

Nathan agreed at once. "You're right, Dennis. I tried to tell her yesterday that she's a good-looking woman."

"Actually, Nathan, I think you'll find Dennis was trying to say I'm a nutter."

Dennis chuckled, Mandy laughed, and Nathan looked bashful.

I gave my new found and suddenly favourite private investigator a gentle smile. "The head injury. It's affected his speech, and you have to learn how to interpret what he's saying, put it in context."

Nathan chuckled. "Whatever he really meant, it sounded right."

I concentrated on Mandy. "Does Paddy know you're here?"

"Yes. I told him I had to come and see you regarding the Selkirk case. He wasn't very pleased, but when the day dawns that me and baby—" she patted her pronounced bump, "— can't handle Paddy Quinn, that's the day we call it a draw."

That was Mandy all over. A determined young woman, one who couldn't be browbeaten even when the browbeater was her boss. We had been friends for many years, though she didn't join the police until long after I had left, and I knew her as well, maybe better, than I knew my own daughter. With just a couple of months to go before the baby's due date, she steadfastly refused to name the father, and had made it clear that she intended bringing up the child on her own.

Nathan elected to comment upon the matter. "Surely you should be on maternity leave this close to your date."

"When I've time. Right now, we're too busy. Besides, what would I do with maternity leave? Sit around the house all day twiddling my thumbs and waiting for junior to let me know she's ready to put in an appearance?"

"You could come and visit me," I said. "Give me a hand with Dennis." Dennis gave a thumbs up to the idea, and I teased Mandy further. "You see. He's all for it. Anything to get a pretty woman dressing and undressing him."

Mandy pulled a face of mock disdain. "Pass." She drank some tea. "Now, come on, the pair of you. I want to know what you know about Fay

Selkirk's murder."

"Nothing," Nathan said. "But we have suspicions, and from my point of view, there may be a link to a ten-year old case involving the same family."

"Bill Duckett," I said.

Maddy chewed her lip. "Yes, Paddy mentioned it yesterday. I checked up after we spoke on the phone last night, Chrissy, and the official verdict was accidental death. Bill Duckett died when the auto lift crushed him. Do you know different?"

I shook my head. "I spoke to Tony Wharrier yesterday, and he was suspicious at the time. I'm dredging the depths of my memory, but I'm sure Dennis was just as suspicious. Their opinion is that Duckett would not be working under that car without the safety locks activated."

Dennis nodded vigorously. "Hook it. Heard herd."

Mandy and Nathan both frowned, and I advised them, "Just ignore him. It's the meds talking."

"No." Dennis tapped my arm. "Hook it. Heard herd."

This time, I frowned. "What are you trying to say, Dennis? Hook it? Do you mean…" I trailed off, dredging my mind for some suitable (and printable) sound-alike.

It was Mandy who rumbled it. "He's trying to say Duckett."

Dennis nodded again. "Heard herd." His eyes burned into us, willing us to understand and eventually the penny dropped.

"Murdered?" I asked, and received more

vigorous nods by return. I turned to the others. "He's saying that Bill Duckett was murdered."

"I gathered that." Mandy shook her head. "I'm sorry, Chrissy, but I need something more than Dennis's say so, and your suspicions. There was no one in that workshop that day. Duckett was on his own, and forensics found no trace of anyone else… Well, obviously they found plenty of traces, but none that shouldn't have been there. There were traces of Janet, Sebastian, drivers from suppliers, even customers, but we accounted for every one of them, and Bill Duckett was alone. Even the guys in the nearby workshops insisted they had seen no one in Duckett's workshop all morning but for Bill himself. I don't care how much Tony Wharrier and Dennis insist on him being a top-notch mechanic, the fact is he made a mistake, something went wrong, and he died as a result." She paused to let her words sink in. "If you and Nathan can bring me anything else, anything which disputes that record, then I'm willing to listen. Other than that, you're wasting your breath."

I was annoyed. No, not annoyed. Frustrated. I knew exactly what Mandy was talking about and she was dead right. A ten-year-old case coming to the fore on nothing more than suspicion and the crazy coincidence that Nathan had discovered in Anita Stocker's novels.

Deliberately changing the subject, I asked, "What can you tell us about Fay Selkirk?"

"Not much. And most of what we do know is under wraps for the time being."

"You quizzed Anita Stocker on the basis of a tip

off."

"An accurate tipoff."

"And the caller?"

"Anonymous."

"Male, female?"

"Male. Hell fire, Chrissy, what are you trying to do to me?"

"Nothing. I'm proving two of my clients innocent, at least of tipping you people off." I toyed with my cup, giving her a moment to calm down. "If the caller was definitely male, it can't have been Val Wharrier or Anita Stocker."

She did calm down, but now she was puzzled. "Why would it be?"

I spent a few moments telling her of Val's visit the previous day and of Anita's Stocker's attitude when we saw her. It did not go down well.

"When we quizzed Stocker she insisted she didn't know who had called us. And to be honest, we weren't that bothered. The moment we accessed her laptop, we knew the call was on the button. That scene in her next novel is a dead ringer for the way we found Fay Selkirk in Hattersley Woods. Why do you think we spent two hours grilling Stocker?"

I had no answer to what I considered a rhetorical question. But Nathan was not short of a response. "And why do you think we're asking about Bill Duckett's death?"

"Heard herd," Dennis commented.

"I'm sure you're right, my friend," Nathan said. He lifted his briefcase to the table, flipped it open and took out a paperback copy of *Crushed* by Anita Stocker. He closed the case, put it back on the wooden decking, and laid the book on the table. "Her first novel. Ten years old now, still a good seller. Have a read of page ten."

While Mandy opened the book and flipped through the pages, Nathan expanded on the previous day's explanation. "One of the women in the office at... at WDIG is a fan of Anita Stocker's work and when she heard that Anita had been questioned, she remembered the opening sequence of this book and was chatting to her colleagues. One of them recognised it as the manner in which Bill Duckett died. The combination of her arrest and this woman's recollection are what set the whole WDIG ball rolling."

Mandy closed the book and pushed it to me, having read the necessary passage. "It means nothing, Nathan. We knew about it ten years ago. It's in the case file. Anita based her first book on what happened to Bill."

Nathan went into the explanation he'd given me the previous day on how the piece could have been written before Bill's death. I left him and Mandy to the game of theoretical tennis, and looked at the book cover.

It gave me the shudders. Not because it was so graphic. I mean, it was horrible. It showed a man in overalls struggling under an auto lift loaded with a car while a shadowy figure looked on. It reminded me of the image of Dennis those animals had sent to me when they were through beating him up, which in turn brought back the anxiety and dread of that terrible Friday evening. That made me tremble. Dennis took my hand for a moment and I wondered if he had noticed my apprehension. I gave him a false smile of reassurance, and focussed on the debate between Nathan and Mandy.

It was Nathan doing most of the talking. "This business of preparing the script well in advance doesn't just apply to Bill Duckett's death, you know. It could also be the case with Fay Selkirk."

"Not so," Mandy retorted. "We checked her laptop, remember. That document was prepared a couple of hours before Fay's body was discovered, and Fay hadn't been dead long when she was found."

He dismissed the argument out of hand. "You want me to show you how that could be done? It's not difficult. You download the file to memory stick. You then wipe the file from the laptop and reboot. When you've done that, you install the file from the memory stick and fool around with it to ensure the date and time it was modified has changed."

Mandy was gobsmacked. I was less surprised but even so, I gaped.

"Your IT guys need to rip that laptop to pieces to ensure it didn't happen. They need to check everything in the event logs, but if she knows what she's doing, she could have taken care of that so you might never know."

"Not her," I argued. "Her son. Sebastian. He's the one who thinks he's an IT expert."

Nathan shrugged. "Whoever. All I'm saying is that you cannot take the document properties at face value. There are ways and means of getting round them."

The conversation was grinding to a halt.

"There is another possibility," I said, and had their immediate attention. "Suppose her machine was hacked?"

Mandy might have been willing to listen, but Nathan doubted it and said so. "Twice? Ten years apart? It doesn't seem likely. I mean, how many different machines has she owned in that time?"

For the first time since I met him, I felt a flurry of irritation with Nathan. "And how do we know that these two are the only killings based on her works? Assuming they were actually based on her novels, that is. You say she's turned out thirty or forty books, Val told me the same thing. How many other killings are there which match her works?"

"None that I'm aware of," Mandy said.

"None in Haxford, you mean. You need to check with someone who knows her work and then run a national search, Mandy. But there is a quicker way of finding out."

"Yes?" Nathan asked.

"Get someone to hack her computer. I know you can't do that, Mandy, but I know someone who could probably introduce us to a hacker."

With a smile, Mandy put her fingers in her ears. "I'm not hearing any of this."

Nathan, on the other hand, encouraged me. "The ball's in your court."

"I took out my phone, called up the directory and pushed the dial button. A minute later, he answered. "Lester. It's Chrissy. And for once, I really do want you."

Chapter Eleven

The Sump Hole was the local soubriquet for the Engine House pub, so named because once upon a time, before my time, of course, a small mill had stood nearby and the pub was located close to what had been the boiler house which stoked the engines which in turn drove the looms.

Situated on Weaver Street just off the western by-pass, and consequently on the outskirts of the town centre, it had never been one of my favourite haunts even in my younger, carefree days. Fights were rare, but they did happen now and then. My deeper doubts about the place stemmed from its location and clientele. It stood so close to the town centre, the major betting shops and the job centre that it attracted the kind of patrons I preferred to avoid. Not that I could always avoid them. As a private eye it was often part of my work to mix with the – ahem – underclass, as they were often described. It was a polite way of saying the Engine House was home to every thief, conman, wheeler dealer, and general layabout Haxford had to offer, and twelve noon on a Thursday saw it packed with many such examples.

After Mandy left, I explained the proposition in detail to Nathan who was doubtful.

"We're chasing up something which might not have happened, and it's gonna cost. That's money. These guys won't give you a receipt, and without it, you can't claim the expenses."

"Suppose it did happen, Nathan?" I asked, and followed it up with a cheeky smile. "I do Dennis's books so I'm well versed in creative accountancy, and I'm perfectly capable of adding the expense in other areas. Anita will never know the difference, and if it clears her name, she's not likely to argue."

He capitulated. "Fair enough. And this Lester Grimes is a capable hacker is he?"

"No. But I'm willing to bet he knows one or two."

I rang Naomi, asking if she could sit with Dennis while I chased up the slender idea. She agreed, and ten minutes later, Nathan and I stepped out of the front door and I aimed the remote at my Diablo. He stopped me.

"We'll take my car. No offence, but it's more comfortable than a converted van."

"It does have rear seats, you know? They're just flattened to accommodate the power wheelchair."

"The seats in my car can be flattened, too, but it's usually for a more pleasurable purpose. I'm in a better position to afford the petrol." He hugged me. "I'm here to help, Chrissy, and if I can do that by standing the expenses, then let me."

I wasn't disposed to argue any further, we climbed into his VW for the drive, first to Haxford Mill, where we picked up Lester, and then to the Engine House.

Whether it was the presence of Nathan, I don't

know but Lester behaved himself in the rear seat of the car. There were none of his usual lewd and suggestive remarks. Instead he concentrated on the man we were about to meet.

"His name's Eddie Myner."

My head half turned towards him, I misheard. "Minor? As in someone who's not old enough yet?"

"No. Myner as in a bloke what digs coal, only it's spelled different."

"Unusual name. Especially considering there are no coal mines in this part of Yorkshire. And how do we spell it?"

"Aye well, happen his granddad came from Doncaster or Barnsley or somewhere, and it's spelled M-Y-N-E-R."

"Hmm. Not even the same as the talking bird. What do you know about him, Lester?"

"Enough. He went through school and learned all about computers but there weren't no vacancies in Haxford, and he didn't wanna move, and he got fed up of filling shelves at CutCost, so he went solo."

"You mean he's unemployed."

"If you wanna get technical, yes. But he makes dosh on the side hacking into things like pay sites. I meanersay, Chrissy, he can get you free access to fillums, telly programmes, and even the naughty sites."

"I don't want to rain on your parade, Lester, or his, but I'm not looking for such dubious entertainment. I need him to do me a favour, and I'll pay him for it."

He grinned. "Oh, aye? Do I get a commission?"

"If you behave yourself, you'll get a free pint.

Just introduce me to him and let me do the talking."

"No problem, but you need to know that he likes to be called Borer."

"Because he bores the socks off you?"

"No. It's because borers bore into the ground, don't they? You know. To dig the coal and diamonds out."

"There are even fewer diamond mines round here than there are coal mines."

Nathan spent most of the journey laughing at the absurd exchange, almost as if he were getting used to Lester Grimes's wayward manner.

When we walked into the pub, I was expecting a teenager, a young geek obsessed with IT and ready to dive into my requirements with all the energy of a footballer determined to take on the world. In fact, Eddie Myner was about forty-five years old. His black hair had all but gone at the front, yet hung down in a ponytail at the back. He was about four stones overweight (that estimate was generous on account of how I wanted him to work for me) clad in a shabby body warmer – as if it wasn't warm enough already – with a dirty, dark green T-shirt underneath. His red-rimmed eyes regarded Nathan and me with suspicion, and I guessed that if Lester had not been there, he would not give us the time of day.

I handed Lester ten pounds, told him to go to the bar and get drinks, a lemonade for me and Nathan – one of us was driving – and whatever he and Myner wanted. Not a single word passed between us, not even between Nathan me, during the interlude and I began to feel awkward when Lester got back with the drinks.

"Borer, this is Chrissy and her mate, Nate. Chrissy, Nate, Borer. They need a favour."

Myner grunted and sipped the head off his beer.

Nathan made the opening announcement. "We're private investigators, Mr Myner—"

"Goodbye." He put down his glass and stood up, ready to leave.

Lester stayed him. "Hang on, buddy, just hang on. They're not looking to nick you. They needs you to do something for them."

With the feeling that Lester could have phrased it better, I nodded. "And we're willing to pay you."

Wearing a face and eyes haunted with suspicion, Myner sat down and took another wet from his glass. A long silence followed, so long that I had to wonder if he was waiting for me to say more, but if so, he wasn't focussed on me. Instead, his eyes wandered around the room pausing here and there to study some man or woman, then coming back to us before going on another tour of the bar.

I was on the point of prompting him, when he beat me to it.

"If anything happens, I don't know neither of you, I never met you, and I'll get a couple of blokes to fill him in." He jerked a stubby thumb in Lester's direction.

Lester laughed. "Come off it, Borer, you don't know enough blokes to fill me in."

There was enough noise in the room to scupper the chance of anyone listening in, but even so I kept my voice down as I took the lead. "Nothing untoward will happen, Mr Myner. I need you to get into a system for me and report back. That's all. It's a private set up. Not linked to any company or organisation. I need to know if it's been hacked, and to find that out, I need you to hack it. Can you do it?"

"Fifty dabs."

Nate reached for his wallet, but I stayed him. "You're paying for the petrol." I took out my purse, retrieved the money from it, and showed it to him, but when he reached for it, I retracted my hand. "When you've done as I ask. Lester will vouch for me."

He glanced at my husband's business partner seeking confirmation. "She's good for it," Lester told him."

Myner shrugged. "What's the operating system, what kind of security is wrapped around it?"

"It's a laptop," I said.

He tutted. "Blooming typical. The operating system, missus. Is it Microsoft, Apple Mac, Android—"

Nathan cut him off. "We don't know. It belongs to a client and she's assured Chrissy that it hasn't been hacked. We're not happy about that and we need to know, not guess."

"Does she know what you're planning?"

"No, and we don't want her to know. Can you do it?"

"Piece of p—"

"Language."

"I was gonna say, piece of pie. Y'see, it doesn't matter how good these programmers think they are, there are always ways of getting in."

From there he proceeded to waffle about slipways, back doors, trapdoors, hidden entries, and for a time I wondered whether he was talking about the adult sites Lester had mentioned. But no, he went on at some length discussing algorithms, Trojans, spikes, router hacks, BIOS, event logs, and so on to such a degree that I wasn't sure what we were discussing. It could have been the latest Brian Cox lecture on the origins of the universe or a dissertation on Greek history. One thing I did decide. I had it right when I said his handle, Borer, had more to do with tedium and putting people to sleep than mining coal or precious minerals.

Eventually, he got down to our requirements.

"Simplest way is to let me send an email masked with your address, and get the punter to click the link. That'll get me into her system and from there, I can check it out. The full shufti will take maybe twenty-four hours, but the unknown is, will she click the link. Most people are not that dumb. Offer them a ten percent cut of eighteen billion dollars from the Nigerian oil ministry and they'll just dump it."

"Do people still try that one?" Lester asked.

"Not often," Myner said. "I was using it as an example."

"To get back to our requirements," I interrupted, determined to stem the danger of wandering off along another pointless and incomprehensible track. "Would it help if I told her to expect the email and click the link?"

"If you can persuade her."

"Then that's what I'll do." I took out my pocket

book and wrote down my email address. "Terms and conditions. Once you've done this and reported back to me, you get rid of everything you've found. You don't keep anything. Yes?"

"No sweat."

"Two, you do not breathe a word to another living soul."

He pointed at Lester. "He's heard everything."

"I have doubts that Lester is alive. Three, you keep us posted on your progress. Text messages will be fine. All right?" I scribbled my phone number down on the same sheet of paper, handed it to him, and gave him the fifty pounds. "If I don't hear from you by six o'clock tomorrow evening, Nathan will have people out looking for you, and they won't be half as gentle as us."

"Or as pretty as Chrissy," Nathan commented.

I couldn't say for Nathan, but my threat was as empty, as his comment was fly, but the combination appeared to work. "You've got a deal, missus."

Myner left, we finished our drinks and Nathan offered Lester a lift back to the mill, but he declined. "I'll have another couple of snifters in here before I go back."

Glad to be out of the place, I got into the passenger seat of Nathan's car and rang Anita. "You'll receive an email from me later today. When you get it, just click the link, please."

"An email? Concerning what?"

Damn. I forgot to give Myner instructions on what to put in the message. "You'll see when you get it, but it's vital that you click the link."

"Isn't that a bit risky? For me, I mean."

I gave her a well-rehearsed, tittery little laugh. "This is from me, Anita, and I'm working for you. You're paying me, remember. Would I put you under any risk?"

"Well, all right. If you say so, Christine."

"Thank you."

Nathan started the engine. "Okay, boss. Where next?"

I liked the way he called me 'boss' but I had to think about our next move. Eventually, I said, "I really should get back and relieve Naomi, but there is another call we can make. The public library."

From the pub, I guided him round the bypass to the other side of town, and the library, a place which became almost a second base during the Graveyard Poisoner investigation, and the place where my good friend, Kim Aspinall worked alongside her current partner, Alden Upley.

Kim and I had been friends for many years. A little air-headed at times, she was between men friends when Alden's wife was murdered. She took pity on him, and he moved into her spare room and not long after that he moved from there into her bed. It surprised me at the time. There was a considerable age gap, and as a couple, they were superficially incompatible, and yet they had lasted seven months, with occasional talk of marriage. Where Kim was a lively woman some years my junior, Alden was a stuffed shirt. Well, that was my opinion of him. He was a stickler for the rules, whereas in Kim's opinion there was only one rule; enjoy life.

On the other hand, both had been permanent

fixtures at the library for more years than I could remember, and if anyone knew anything about the background to Bill Duckett's untimely and – to me – suspicious death it would be them.

I was right. I introduced Nathan to her, spotted her eyes glazing over with lust, and then told her why we were there. The moment I mentioned Bill Duckett, Kim invited us to the little staff room behind the counter, where she made tea, and while Alden stood at the door, keeping one eye on the counter, one ear on our conversation, she told me the tale, which basically coincided with Tony Wharrier's account.

"Tony assured us that Duckett was a top man, and there's no way he would have been using that lift without setting the safety locks," I told her.

"I remember my boyfriend at the time saying summat the same," Kim said, "but according to the filth – Paddy Quinn had just been promoted to inspector, and he was the top dog on the investigation – that's what happened. They said there was no trace of anyone else in the workshop at the time. The workers in the units nearby said they'd seen and heard nothing. Course, he'd been dead for hours when they found him, and no one's really sure what time he clocked out."

"Dennis also told me that the son, Sebastian, used to help his father out now and then."

"Yeah, but they reckon he was in college all morning and during the afternoon he was out with some lass somewhere." Kim's faced soured. "Have you met him? Crikey, talk about I do love me. He hit on me once over, you know. Just after that git did a runner on me."

The 'git' in question was Wayne Peason, Kim's live-in partner who walked out on her. A year after his disappearance, she pulled Alden into her nest.

And talking of Alden, he chimed in at that point. "I had to warn Sebastian Duckett about his conduct on several occasions, Christine. Particularly towards the women using the library."

We were getting side-tracked. "Thinking on Bill Duckett, were there any issues with his business that you know of?"

Kim laughed. "You mean like Jack Frogshaw threatening him or summat?"

Jack Frogshaw was a man who fancied himself as the local criminal mastermind. He was a little shady and had a reputation for loan sharking on a small scale, but he was also transparent and well-known to the police, and that made him less of a mastermind than my granddaughter, Bethany, and she was only three years old.

"That kind of thing," I said, agreeing to Kim's question.

"The Bill Duckett I knew – and I didn't know him well – was big and strong, a bit like your Dennis only fatter, and he would have chewed Frogshaw up and spit the bones out for his dog to chew on."

My phone tweeted to announce an incoming message. It was from an unidentified number. *I'm in*, it said. I assumed it was from Eddie Myner. If not, it could only be a burglar tormenting me after breaking into our home, finding Dennis incapacitated, and helping himself to our goods and chattels.

A second later, the phone rang. It was Anita Stocker, I cut it off, put the phone into flight mode and dropped it back in my bag.

"Anita never said anything about a dog. And neither did Mandy," I said.

"Janet got shot of it after Bill died. She never did like the mutt. Well, she's worth a flaming fortune, isn't she, and as toffee nosed as her kid? Spends half the year in the Canary Islands or somewhere."

"Southern Spain, actually."

Nathan homed in on the dog. "You say Anita didn't like the dog. Do you know if it was with Mr Duckett that morning?"

"Definitely," Alden replied. "It was the dog's barking which eventually alerted others that something was wrong."

"And yet it took them hours to find him?" Nathan sounded as if he didn't believe it, and neither did I.

Alden nodded gravely. "That is the story, Christine. I found it odd, too, but that was the official police account."

***

The clock in Nathan's car read a few minutes to one when he started the engine. He made no attempt to move the vehicle. Instead, he half turned to face me. "Congratulations, Chrissy. You seem to have come round to my way of thinking."

I chewed my lip. "It's beginning to look as if you're right. I'm sorry if I sounded sceptical yesterday. About the link between the two killings, I mean. After I heard Val's account, I had my doubts about Bill Duckett's death anyway. What's this business with the dog? It seemed important to you."

He didn't reply immediately. It was as if he was trying to work out the simple way of putting it. Or perhaps he hadn't actually sorted it out in his mind.

A few moments later, he was ready, and suggested, "Let's make some bold assumptions. Bill Duckett is at work. His wife doesn't like the dog so he takes it with him. The dog's quite happy at the workshop. Someone turns up, there's perhaps an argument, perhaps not. Mr X knocks Bill out, places him under the auto lift, switches off locks, and sets it going so that it comes down and crushes Bill." Nathan's eyes burned into me. "Why didn't the dog bark? Why didn't it go for Bill's attacker? When Bill and Mr X were fighting, I mean."

The question had me on the back foot. I ran it through my mind and came up with various answers.

"Maybe the dog was trained not to bark, and later on, it got hungry, needed a wee, or got fed up of being alone with no one to pay it any attention. Since we don't know the dog, we don't know why it didn't bark."

"Very clever, but there's a simpler solution. The dog didn't bark because it knew Mr – or Mrs X."

I felt deflated. It was so obvious when I thought about it. "Why didn't I think of that?"

Nathan laughed, and placed a hand on my thigh. "Anita is your client, and she's paying you not to think of things like that." He removed his hand and slipped the transmission into 'drive', and asked,

"Home?"

I was slightly distracted by the way his hand connected with my thigh, and my head was a confusion of excitement and suspicion, so it was several seconds before I answered. "Oh. Yes. Please. Naomi's a good girl, but I can't leave her with Dennis for the whole day."

Chapter Twelve

With the nurse not due until the following day, when she would make her final visit of the week, Naomi had helped Dennis onto the sun lounger, where he was sound asleep, but lying the wrong way round, his back flat to the mattress, a pillow supporting his head and neck, his legs raised by the tilt on the lounger's back support.

"It was how he preferred to be," Naomi explained.

"It's good. As you know, he needs to have his legs raised for so long every day." I offered her tea, but she excused herself, saying she had to get Bethany home, and left me on the decking, alone with Nathan.

I sorted out soft drinks for us, and as I joined him, he asked, "What do you know about Sebastian Duckett, Stocker, whatever he wants to call himself?"

"Not much. I met him for the first time yesterday, and I took an instant dislike to him." I chuckled. "Exactly the opposite to the way I felt about you." My remark wasn't intended to encourage him or lead him on, but I worried for a moment that Nathan might see it that way, and I waited for him to comment. When he said nothing, I went on. "Narcissist. He can't walk past a mirror without checking it to ensure he comes up to his idea of perfection, and since that idea is him, the mirror never lies. He also fancies himself as a computer expert, but his idea of expertise is to rely on antivirus and anti-malware packages. That's why we've just been to see our friend Myner. Both he and Anita say that she employs him as her security man, and she was at pains to point out that if and when he chooses to marry, he will take over the house, and she'll move into the granny flat. When she moves to Spain every winter, he goes with her, and he freely admits that he takes girlfriends along." I shrugged. "That's it. You now know as much about Sebastian Stocker as I do."

Nathan appeared to be deep in thought, and he did not respond immediately. Dennis stirred, I went over to him, but by the time I got there, he was asleep again, and I returned to the table.

"Are you thinking it could be him as opposed to Anita? Or even both of them?"

Nathan gave a short sigh. "I don't know. It's possible. All I know for sure is that I have suspicions about Bill Duckett's death, and the knowledge that there was a dog in the workshop, something which no one has ever mentioned before, has only deepened my suspicions. As I said in the car, it may be that the dog knew the intruder, which was why it didn't bark. Who would that dog know well enough to remain silent? Three candidates: Bill himself, Anita, and Sebastian." He took a long swallow of cola. "I think I really need to talk to him, and I'd also like to speak to Anita. Can you fix up a meeting?"

Now it was my turn to register doubts. "She's not an easy proposition, Nathan. She values her privacy. I mean, you haven't seen where she lives… Have you?"

"I have the address, obviously, and I've seen pictures online. The middle of nowhere, isn't it?"

"A wonderful but isolated place. You can't see anything for miles around, other than the moors."

He nodded at Dennis. "Could you arrange someone to look after your husband?"

"I can ask Hazel from next door, but I have to warn you, if we turned up unannounced, Anita will kick off."

He gave me a lopsided, easy smile. "Leave that to me. I can handle women."

I took out my smartphone, rang Hazel, and she agreed to come round right away. In fact, it took her the thick end of ten minutes to get there, and her limp, which had always been obvious, looked worse.

"Flaming hips. Wait while you get to my age, Chrissy. You'll know about it." She beamed on Nathan. "And who's this? The toy boy getting his feet under the table while Dennis is incapable?"

I laughed. "What else would a woman like me do, Hazel? Nathan, this is my wonderful next door neighbour, Hazel McQuarrie. Hazel, this is Nathan Evanson, a fellow private investigator." I got to my feet. "Let me get you a cuppa."

"Summat cold would be preferable, Chrissy. Lemonade or something."

I nipped through the conservatory to the kitchen,

dropped a couple of ice cubes in an empty glass, and filled it with lemonade, then turned back to join them.

Hazel was one of those friendly, chatty neighbours, the kind of woman who could make you feel welcome and comfortable in a matter of seconds.

"It's only yesterday, Chrissy, you were asking me whether going away with Dennis would do any good. Well, let me tell you summat, a week away with this fella would do you a lot more good. I'll look after Dennis for you."

I put on a sheepish grin. Hazel's announcement was too close to some of the recent meanderings of my febrile mind.

Nathan, on the other hand, rose to Hazel's bait. "I'm game if you are, Chrissy."

I wagged a disapproving finger at him. "We're in the middle of an investigation, Nathan. Let's not get distracted. Hazel, can you cope if we shoot off for an hour or two?"

"Take all the time you want, lass." She cackled. "I always liked it slow and steady."

It was with a feeling of slight bewilderment that I climbed into the passenger seat of Nathan's VW. Why was everyone putting the obvious, but wrong interpretation on this man and me? Ours was a professional relationship, and any daydreams I might have of anything different, were just that. Daydreams. And to be fair, although some of Nathan's remarks were flattering, a little cheeky, the closest he'd come to making advances was a hand on my thigh, but I interpreted that as a matey rather than mating gesture.

With me, guiding him, it took twenty minutes to reach the moorland plateau where Hilly Farm could be seen in the distance.

"Wow." Nathan's surprise sounded genuine. "Talk about lonely. Fantastic when the weather's like this, but it must be hell in the winter. Do the council send gritters out here just for her?"

"They send snowploughs and gritters, but it's not for her. Believe it or not, this is actually a main-ish road to Manchester, and it has to be kept clear, or as clear as it can be. Mind you, we haven't had anything like a serious winter for years. We tend to get a few days of snow, and that's it. Even then, it's only light snow."

A few minutes later, he parked behind the Range Rover and Volvo. We climbed out, and as we approached the front door, Sebastian appeared.

"Well, well, well, if it isn't Mrs Capper. And who's this? Your boyfriend?"

If I found him irritating, I was not alone. Nathan took an obvious and instant dislike to him. "I'm another private investigator, Mr... Is it Stocker or Duckett?"

Sebastian did not appear fazed. "I prefer Stocker. And what do you want, Mr private eye?"

"To speak to both you and your mother, and before you start giving me any more backchat, I represent WDIG, your mother's insurers, the company that paid out on your father's death."

"You suspect fraud? You think the old man's still alive and we've got him hidden in the attic? You'd better come in, but I have to warn you, my old queen isn't in the best of moods. Don't blame me if you go away with some bits missing and singing in a falsetto voice."

To my relief, Nathan chose not to get into the macho-macho argument, and ushered me in before following and leaving Sebastian to close the door.

Stocker, the younger, was right. Anita was in a blazing mood and greeted us appropriately.

"I tried to ring you earlier, I couldn't get an answer. I need some explanations from you. And who is this?"

Nathan moved forward and offered his hand. Anita refused to shake it, but my temporary partner was not put out by her blanking him. "Nathan Evanson, private investigator, and as I've just explained to your son, I'm working on behalf of WDIG."

A frown crossed her face. "My insurers?"

"That's correct, Mrs Stocker. And it concerns your late husband's death ten years ago."

From behind us, Sebastian chuckled. "It's all right, Mum. The game's obviously up, so I'll nip upstairs and get Dad to come down and confess."

For a horrible moment, I thought he was being serious. I mean, was everyone absolutely sure the dead man was Bill Duckett? The look of fury on Anita's face told me another story.

She was still speaking to Nathan. "He's dead. It's been ten years. WDIG paid out as they were obliged to."

"Except that with the murder of Fay Selkirk a couple of days ago, and your manuscript mirroring her death, the question of your husband's demise has come up. I'll be frank, Mrs Stocker, and—"

"The policy was valid, even if it was murder," Anita interrupted.

"Yes, we know. However, if it was murder, the two prime suspects are you and your son, and if that was the case, claiming against your husband's insurers could be interpreted as fraud. You could go to prison. Correction, you would go to prison, for Bill's murder, but you'd also be charged with fraud."

I've often wondered about the final straw breaking the camel's back. There were many times in life when I'd reached my limit, and in one instance, shortly after The Incident, I launched myself at the chief suspect. I was happily beating him up when the police pulled me off.

I was reminded of it when Anita rushed Nathan and began to beat her fists into his chest, screaming obscenities as she did so. I was about to intervene when Nathan caught her wrists and guided her back to her seat.

Then Sebastian waded in. He grabbed Nathan's shoulder, spun him round and hissed, "Get your filthy paws off my mother." He threw a punch and I cringed, waiting for Nathan to sink to the carpet.

It didn't happen. Nathan grabbed Sebastian's fist as it came in, and no one was more surprised than the younger man. He struggled against Nathan's grip. Pointless. For all his bulging biceps and six pack, he was no match for Nathan.

"Twenty-two years in the military police, Mr Stocker. I've taken bigger than you. Now do us all a favour and sit down with your mother, and behave yourself or I might forget that there are ladies present."

For me, speaking as a private eye, this was awe-inspiring. I'd had my share of confrontations, much though I tried to avoid them, but in this case, Nathan had – in my opinion – sparked it off. Whether he expected a physical reaction, I couldn't say, but it was obvious that he was more than capable of handling such incidents, and I guessed that the psychology behind his putative accusation, was designed to give him control.

Sebastian sat on the settee, reached out and took his mother's hand. Both Stockers blazed with impotent fury and Nathan move round to stand in front of the fireplace, where he could look on them both.

"No one is accusing either of you of anything, but the question has to be asked, particularly because on the day of Bill's death, neither of you could adequately explain your whereabouts, and as Mrs Capper and I learned earlier today, your late husband had a dog with him in the workshop, and yet no one can recall the dog barking until later that day, several hours after Bill died. At least that's what we've been told. If you can satisfy me as to your whereabouts during the day, I will report back to WDIG, and you will hear no more of the matter."

"It's ten flaming years ago, you idiot," Anita snapped. "I can't remember where I was. I was probably out shopping in Haxford during the morning, and I was here later in the afternoon when the police came and brought the damned dog back."

"Our information is you got rid of the dog, too,

Anita," I said.

It was Sebastian who answered. "My mother doesn't like dogs. She never did. That's why Dad took the animal to the workshop with him. Sabre was quite happy with the old man. And before you brand us as totally callous, we didn't have the dog put to sleep. George Ibble took him, and as far as I know, Sabre is still with George."

Nathan ignored the final remarks, and demanded, "Then why didn't he bark when your father was attacked, Mr Stocker?"

Although the incident with Nathan had unsettled Sebastian, he was in complete control when he answered the question. "Because my father wasn't attacked, Mr Evanescent, or whatever your name is. He was crushed under the auto lift. It was an accident."

Nathan was making little progress, so I took over. "We have been given information, Sebastian, to the effect that your father would never have forgotten to set the safety locks. He was too good a mechanic."

"He was an excellent auto engineer," Sebastian agreed, "but he was like any other man his age. Half his mind on the job, the other half probably listening to the radio, and he forgot. It wouldn't be the first time I'd found him working under it without the locks set."

I left it to Nathan. "All right, let's assume that is the case. Can you tell me where you were on that day, Mr Stocker?"

"I called at the workshop during the morning. There was always a bit of an argument between me and the old man because I wouldn't work with him full-time."

I recalled Simon, having the same argument with Dennis when he was about the age Sebastian would have been at the time of his father's death.

"From there, I went into Haxford, and trapped off with a young woman. We spent the afternoon in Hattersley Woods, and don't ask me what we were doing... although, maybe you should ask. At your age, you've probably forgotten how to do it."

The snide remark was designed to get under Nathan's skin, but it didn't work. Well, it did, but it was me it irritated, and I felt obliged to respond. "Why is it that you brats think you invented it?"

He gave me that insouciant, narcissistic smile of superiority. "I don't think that, Mrs Capper. I just think we've improved on what you had."

With the private thought that it would not take much effort to improve upon what I had at the moment, I kept my mouth shut and once again, left it to Nathan, who addressed Anita.

"I'll repeat, Mrs Stocker. No one is accusing you of anything, but the matter is open to question, and it's been complicated by the similarity of Fay Selkirk's murder to the opening chapter of your next novel. Once we're satisfied that neither you nor your son are involved, I'll make my report to WDIG, and you will probably receive a formal apology from them. For now, we'll bid you good day."

"Not so fast," Anita insisted. She turned her fiery eyes upon me. "You sent me an email. I clicked on the link, and it didn't take me anywhere. Five minutes later, my antivirus software flashed up a warning that someone was trying to get into my system."

I put on a convincing frown. "That's odd. I did wonder why I hadn't received a reply. Did your software stop the hacker?"

Sebastian took over. "We're not sure. I ran a full scan on the system, and there doesn't appear to be any damage done, but the antivirus package did flag up a Trojan which might let hackers in."

"And I never did find out where the link would take me," Anita insisted.

And I hadn't given it any thought. As I spoke, I was making it up on the spot. "It was something and nothing. Just a query on Bill's death, and I think we've cleared that up now."

Remember the old phrase, if looks could kill? Right then, if it were possible, I would be pinned to the wall by the daggers coming from her eyes.

Nathan and I came out into the afternoon sun, and as we climbed into his car, he asked, "George Ibble?"

"Sheep farmer. Well, I say sheep farmer. He was. These days he raises them for shows as much as meat. He also trains dogs, and he's won plenty of prizes for both the sheep and his dogs. He's a heck of a nice man, and if they wanted rid of this dog, George wouldn't hesitate."

"Should we call on him?"

"There's no need. I know George well, and I can ring him. He'll confirm one way or the other."

"Okay. Your opinion?"

I shrugged. "It's still up for question, isn't it?

Both of them had ample opportunity to get to the workshop and deal with Bill, but they were quite vehement in denying it."

He started the engine, took a couple of shunts to turn the car round, and as he drove back along the bumpy track, said, "With a couple of hundred thousand pounds at stake, I'd deny it just as vehemently, too."

Chapter Thirteen

Half a mile along the road, there was a rough layby on the right and to my surprise, Nathan pulled in, and shut the engine down. He threw off his seatbelt, and opened the door. "Forgive me, Christine, I need to try and clear my head a little."

I took my smartphone from my bag, and as he climbed out, I said, "No problem. Nothing like the fresh air of the moors to blow away the cobwebs. I'll give George Ibble a ring, and then join you."

He wandered off along a narrow path which led into the grass, and I spent the next few minutes on the phone to George, who confirmed that he had taken Sabre, a golden retriever, from the Ducketts.

"I had him put to sleep a couple of years ago, Chrissy," he told me. "He was an old dog. Placid temperament and well-behaved, and of course, it didn't take me long to train him properly, but hip dysplasia and bone cancer left him in a lot of pain. Euthanasia was kinder. Never a step I take lightly, but a decision you have to make when the time's right."

We spent another couple of minutes chatting. He asked after Dennis, I gave him appropriate assurances, and then rang off. Dropping the phone in my bag, I looked out through the driver's window, and saw Nathan, a couple of hundred yards along the path, scuffing his feet in the grass either side.

If I'd known what was about to happen, I don't know that I would have left the car, but as I've said on many occasions, the lack of ability to see into the future is, in many ways, a godsend.

I climbed out of the car, and walked quickly along the path, to catch up with him. He was still wandering slowly away from me, and I couldn't work out what was wrong. The confrontation with Anita and Sebastian? The complexities of the case before us, if indeed, there was a case? For sure, he was quieter since we left the Stockers' place; moodier, more introspective. Or maybe he just fancied a walk on the moors.

I was slightly out of breath when I caught up with him, and gasped, "I've just spoken to George, and he confirmed the tale Sebastian told us about the dog. He also confirmed, that the dog was well mannered, well-behaved, and that might well explain why he didn't bark until a few hours had elapsed."

Nathan grunted. "That doesn't get us much further forward, does it?"

Again, I could sense the mood upon him. "What is it, Nathan? What's bothering you? Are you worried about your cut of the money WDIG might recoup? Are you concerned that they won't get it back because there were never any questions to answer about Bill Duckett's death?"

He pulled in a deep breath. "No. It's nothing like that." He turned to face me. "It's you."

For the briefest of instants, I wondered what I'd done wrong, but I didn't have time to think about it before his arms came around me, pulled me close to him, and he bent his head to fasten his lips onto mine.

I resisted, but only for a fraction of a second. When he placed a hand over my left breast, I felt the first stirrings, and when his hands roamed lower at the back and began to bunch up and raise my skirt, I suddenly thought, any second now, he'll be boldly going where no man (other than Dennis) has gone before... Well, not for many years anyway.

Thoughts of Dennis brought a vision of him to my mind's eyes. Not a Dennis fully fit, and ready to take on the world, or even tackle the car owners of Haxford, but a Dennis unconscious on the floor of his workshop, his legs broken, his skull fractured. More images came to me. Dennis laid in a hospital bed, legs bandaged and raised, head bandaged, eyes open, barely able to communicate, his memory of himself, of me, of our life and family gone.

The hem of my skirt was climbing. I reached down and removed his hand, broke the kiss, pressed him gently back, and stood away from him. "I'm sorry. I can't. I wouldn't." I allowed several seconds of silence. "Dennis. You know."

Nathan came alongside me and put his arm around my shoulder. For one fleeting moment, I thought I was in serious trouble. I'd handled my share of sexual assault complaints when I was with the police but I never thought the day would dawn when I became a complainant. I prepared to fight him off, or at least make the attempt, but I needn't have worried. There was no intimacy in Nathan's move. It was more about comfort.

"No. It's me who should apologise," he admitted. "I mistook some of your words. How you liked me and didn't like Sebastian Stocker, and I, er... suddenly felt an overwhelming desire for you. I'm sorry."

Exerting rigid control over my tumultuous feelings, I said, "Take me home, please."

The journey took twenty minutes, but to me it seemed like a lifetime. I was not annoyed but confused. The kiss lasted less than half a minute, but during that time, I felt my desire rising, and even if I excused myself on the grounds of Dennis' condition and the anguish, the pressure it put me under, it was not right. It went against everything I believed in.

No words passed between us until he reversed into the drive at Bracken Close, stopped the engine and made eye contact. "Do we carry on with the case?"

"I..." I was still unsure of how I should react. I wanted to say 'No. I don't want to take the risk of seeing you again because I don't know if I could stop myself,' but beneath and behind the incident out on the moors, we were professionals, and we were supposed to behave as such. "Come to the house tomorrow. Make it late morning. I have shopping to deal with. Let's say half past eleven, and we'll take it from there."

He agreed, I climbed out of the car, and as he drove off I made my way into the house, along the hall, through the kitchen and conservatory, and out into the back garden where I found Naomi watching over Bethany, who was teasing Cappy the Cat.

"Mrs McQuarrie's gone home, Chrissy. Dennis is back in bed. He was all but exhausted when I helped him there."

I nodded. I still did not trust myself to say anything.

It's one of those things they don't teach you in school. Words have only a small part to play in communication. According to my reading on the subject, eighty percent of our understanding is silent: body language, tone of voice, inflection, facial masks. Without realising it, most of us are experts in the matter, and so was Naomi. One look at me, and she knew there was something wrong.

"What is it, Chrissy? What's happened?"

"Nothing. It's nothing." Even to me, I did not sound convincing.

"I was always told that mothers can tell when their daughters are hiding something. Trouble is, daughters can tell when mothers are hiding things, too. Now come on what is it? You can tell me."

I could contain myself no longer. I told her what had happened and she immediately misinterpreted it. "Right. Sexual harassment. I'll have him for that. I'll ring Simon, and we'll have him—"

I cut her off. "No, no, no. You don't understand." The words came out in a torrent. "He didn't force himself on me. He didn't assault me. He made the first move, yes, but I stopped him before it went too far. It's not that that bothers me, Naomi. It's me. Just for a moment, I was ready to do it. I didn't want to. I've never done that. It isn't right. There's no way I could betray Dennis like that. But it was there in my mind. The temptation. I was so near to…" I tailed off and swallowed a large lump in my throat.

She gave me a hug, and when she next spoke her anger had gone, and she brimmed with the self-assurance of someone who understood people, someone who understood me. "Maybe you should have let him. The stress you've been under this last month or more, something like that would do you no end of good, and no one would be any wiser, would they? Certainly not Dennis."

I disagreed. "It's not me, Naomi. I wasn't brought up like that. Throw away thirty years of faith for a quickie in the grass with a man I've known two days? It just isn't me."

I felt the situation was reversed from what it should be. She was a young woman, married to my son, and if anyone needed advice, observations on life, it should be her looking to me.

"It was obvious from the first time I saw you and him together that you liked him," she said. "You should have just laid back and let him take you to heaven, Chrissy. Just for a few minutes."

I shook my head. "I like him. I don't love him."

"What's love got to do with it? It's sex, Chrissy, and when you bury your worries in horizontal exercise for twenty minutes or half an hour, it's known as sublimation. It takes you away from the here and now and all the crap that goes with issues like Dennis."

Perhaps it was a twenty-first century attitude, but to me it sounded more like the sixties, a decade I missed, and the old mantra; tune in, turn on, drop out. "Dennis is not an issue. He's my husband, so I don't see it like that."

"No, nor me most of the time," she said, contradicting her last words, "but I'm looking at a woman I love very dearly, a woman I respect more than my own mother, and what I can see is a woman on the edge. You need some serious you time, Chrissy, and that quickie in the long grass counts as you time. Still, it's history now, isn't it. I assume you'll no longer be working with him."

I shook my head. "We're in the middle of a complex case, and it probably needs the both of us. I'm not sure, but I do think we'll have to carry on working together."

She gave me a lascivious smile. "In that case, the next time he shows up and kisses you, leave your pants off. He'll get the message."

I realised she was trying to lighten the mood but her suggestion did nothing for me other than make me wonder whether I would actually do just that.

***

Friday morning dawned with more of the same, unremitting sunshine and heat. I dragged my weary bones out of bed at half past seven when Dennis buzzed me in need of the commode. To my surprise when I got there, he'd already used it, having got himself out of bed and all he needed me to do was empty it.

He wheeled himself from the bedroom to the kitchen where I set him up with breakfast and sat with him working my way through a cup of strong coffee. My actions were those of an automaton, a robot working to a pre-defined and familiar program.

"High ketting petter," he muttered through a mouthful of Weetabix and it took me a moment to translate it as 'I'm getting better'.

I gave him a weak smile. "Yes, you are, love." I was tempted to tell him what had happened the previous day, but I decided against it. I was having a rough time of things, but he was having it worse, it wouldn't be fair to burden him with more worries. The knowledge that a man I was working with had the hots for me might set him back. "I have to nip out this morning, Dennis. Only CutCost, and I should be back by eleven o'clock. I'm expecting Nathan."

"You aunty pants." Fancy man, that meant, and he grinned to show he was only joking.

I didn't react. Had he noticed? Had some sixth sense told him of the previous afternoon? Or had he taken his prompts from listening to the likes of Hazel McQuarrie and her teasing? I discounted Naomi. She would not say anything to him.

"We're in the middle of a complicated case, Dennis. I have to work with him and I have to look after you."

"Heck it easy. Snow prob." That was simple to translate. 'Take it easy, it's no problem'.

I'd decided against ordering online for this week. I needed a dose of normality and the weekly visit to CutCost was a part of that.

It's one of those anomalies that Friday, post-rush hour, is one of the best times for getting to and getting round a massive supermarket like CutCost. I was there for half past nine and ready for coming out again by ten past ten, and as I came away from the checkout, I noticed a table littered with second hand books, all priced at £1 and the proceeds would go to an animal shelter located between Haxford and Huddersfield. I'd probably passed it scores of times. What took my eye was a dog-eared paperback of *Squelched*, by Anita Stocker.

Considering my reaction to the brief extract of *Utter Carnage* Val had shown me, I guessed it would not be my kind of tale, but it would make for interesting research, and at a pound, I could hardly go wrong, so I paid for it, and made my way home. By half past ten, with Dennis back in bed, I was at the kitchen table, a cup of tea in front of me, and checking out page ten which gave a lurid description of how a young couple were thrown naked and alive into a giant pulping machine in a paper mill. Out of pure interest, I Googled the prospect and it came up with a real case from Greater Manchester several years earlier.

Excitement gripped me. I needed Nathan here ASAP and that's when I learned I had no number for him. We had never spoken over the phone and when he showed me his business card, he put it back in his shirt pocket. I rang the Haxford Arms and they said he was out. No problem, I Googled the number for WDIG and after explaining the situation to the switchboard, they put me through to their senior claims assessor.

It was five minutes of confusion as I detailed the case Nathan and I were working on, and when I finally got the message across, she was befuddled.

"Nathan Evanson you're saying?"

"That's right. He's one of your preferred private investigators."

"If he was, I'd know him, and I've never heard of him. I don't know who you're dealing with, but he's nothing to do with this company."

Chapter Fourteen

I had never felt so foolish. This big, all-singing, all-dancing private eye who boasted contacts with a large insurance company, but he came seeking out the help of a hick, small town nosy parker like me. Looking back on it, nothing rang true.

I should have guessed. Hadn't I asked why he was staying in a hotel when Bradford was less than twenty miles away? Was I really so enraptured by his charm and good looks that it scrambled my logic circuits?

Hindsight is rarely of any use, but in this instance I found it a great comfort. Not because Mr Bigger Liar than Tom Pepper had been leading me by the nose, but because I'd rejected his advances. As I confessed to Naomi, I had come close to letting down both my guard and my underwear, but my ingrained fidelity overcame the fleeting desire for relief, and by relief I don't mean the obvious kind, the immediate, sexual gratification such an incident would give me. I mean relief from the day-to-day pressure of dealing with a life gone sour. My faith in my marriage assumed its rightful place, taking precedence over the desire for that escape, and I stopped him.

If I was confused in the aftermath, alternately

praising and castigating myself for not finding the courage to go through with it, my head was clear enough now. Instead, I boiled with anger, and the object of my fury was not there. But he would come. He had promised he would be there for half past eleven, and when he turned up, he would learn that you did not cross Christine Capper.

Somewhere beneath this increasing anger was the mystery of who and what he really was, and it didn't take me long to work out the answer.

Organised crime.

I don't know what kind of shady dealings were going on, but I would bet that Bill Duckett was up to his spanners and spark plugs in it. Maybe creating what were known as ringers: stolen cars with the engine numbers altered, registration and number plates changed. It was the ideal criminal activity for a top class mechanic. If that was the case, Nathan Evanson (if that was his real name) had been sent not to learn the secret of Bill Duckett's death, because the chances were he already knew. No, he was sent to make sure it remained buried. Whoever was paying Nathan must have got nervous after the murder of Fay Selkirk and the way in which it automatically implicated Anita Stocker in whatever was going on. The stupid woman (stupid from their point of view) had written the poor girl's murder as the opening to her next novel, and if (what did I mean if?) Anita was hand in glove with these people, privy to whatever crooked game her husband had been playing, they would be monitoring her work. So they sent Nathan along to ensure that the death of Bill Duckett didn't get drawn into the current police investigation.

And yet, it didn't make complete sense. Throughout the last few days, he had all but confirmed my suspicion that Bill Duckett was murdered. So why…

And then it dawned on me. The memory of his hands wandering over my bottom, gathering up my skirt, provided the answer. He would create a false sense of security, then he would take and satisfy me, and then he would present me with Hobson's choice. Keep my mouth shut about Bill Duckett or my husband, my son and precious daughter-in-law, my whole family, all of Haxford and as many daily tabloids as were interested would get to know just how I liked to abandon my disabled husband and enjoy myself with other men.

What would that do to me? My putative career as a radio agony aunt would be terminated before it got properly going. My predecessor, Lizzie Finister had been fired for less. My credibility as a vlogger and blogger would be shot, and any chance I had of picking up clients as a private investigator would be laughed at. I would be held up to public ridicule, exposed as a cheating wife, a woman not to be trusted.

The scenario spurred my rage to even greater heights. I wanted Nathan Evanson in front of me right there and then so I could punch, kick, tear out his eyes, pound him to a bloody pulp.

He was late arriving and I don't know how I got through the next forty-five minutes. I was running on automatic pilot, cleaning, dusting, running the Dyson over the carpet, my nerves frayed by boiling rage until they were near to breaking point.

And then, at last, with the clock reading 11:45, his car pulled up outside.

How should I react? Greet him with a smile, put him off his guard, make him a cup of tea, and then throw it in his face?

I remained impassive as I let him in and led him to the kitchen. I indicated that he should sit at the table, while I made tea, and then joined him.

He must have sensed something was amiss when I didn't opt for the conservatory or the garden, but I didn't want to risk any neighbours overhearing the coming battle.

"How are we this morning, Chrissy?"

"I'm glad you asked that, Nathan. I'm furious…" I paused to ensure he got the next message with maximum force. "With you."

He chuckled. "Oh dear. What have I done now? I mean, if it's yesterday afternoon—"

I cut him off. "That's only a tiny part of it. You've been lying to me since the moment we met." I took some satisfaction from his grim puzzlement. "I needed to speak to you an hour ago, but of course, you've never rung me since we met, so I didn't have your number. I rang the Haxford Arms, but you were out. So I rang WDIG, and guess what? They've never heard of you. But you know that already, don't you? You are a liar. You're up to your greasy neck in this business, and if you didn't actually murder Bill Duckett, you know who did, and you're making sure that people keep their mouths shut about it. That's why you tried to get into my pants yesterday. Once you'd had me, you could blackmail me into shutting up too."

"Hold on, hold on. You're getting this all wrong."

"Am I? I'm good at jumping to conclusions, but this time, they're the only logical conclusions. Or have you got some other fanciful story?"

He appeared calm, collected, and reached inside his jacket, and in that moment, I knew how big a mistake I had made. I was dead. He would pull out a gun and shoot me. And after me, it would be Dennis's turn. I trembled. Why did I have to open my big mouth? I'd already worked out that he was probably linked to whichever criminal gang Bill Duckett worked for, so why hadn't I realised what he might do when I confronted him? Why didn't I use my head and call the police when I first twigged everything an hour ago?

I closed my eyes, waiting for the click of a hammer drawn back. I would not hear the shot. Bullets travel faster than sound. Even across such a short space, I would be making my peace with God long before the crack of a pistol could reach my ears.

Should I beg? Never. It would be pointless. He may very well have been the man who killed Bill Duckett, and he wouldn't have listened then, so he wouldn't listen to me now. Besides, Chrissy Capper never begs. Not just not very often, but never.

The gunshot never came. Instead, he said, "Go on. Have a look."

I opened my eyes to find a small, leather wallet on the table. Packed with money, no doubt. So he was going to try buying me off first. Some chance.

They say everyone has their price but I was the exception that helped prove the rule.

He must have guessed the way my mind was working. "Please, Chrissy. Take a look."

I reached a tentative hand, took the wallet, opened it, and my fear dissipated. Inside was his driver's licence and photograph of a little girl not much older than Bethany. The licence declared him to be *Nathan Kalinsky*.

I stared from the wallet to him and back again. I laid the wallet on the table and picked up my beaker. I noticed the way my hands were shaking as I lubricated my parched palate.

He reached into his jacket again, and came out with a business card. It was different to the one he'd shown me when we first met. This one identified him more fully. *Kalinsky Investigations*, and bore an address in York.

"I really am a private investigator. It's just that I'm from York, not Bradford. No point ringing the number, of course. It'll only bring you to my phone." He took out the smartphone and held it up. "But there is one thing you can do. Ring the Yorkshire Police Divisional HQ in York and ask to speak to Superintendent Jacobs. We go back a long way, me and Brian, and even though he thinks I'm a pain in the butt, he'll vouch for me. Here, let me give you the number—"

"I'll find the number myself," I said. If it sounded like I didn't trust him, it was because I didn't trust him.

I Googled the number for Yorkshire's divisional HQ, and dialled. After some debate with the switchboard they put me through to Detective Superintendent Jacobs, and we had a bit of a chat, the upshot of which was that he could vouch for Nate Kalinsky. "A right pain in the bum, but a good man, Mrs Capper."

I killed the call and confronted Nathan. "All right, so you're telling me part of the truth. What are you doing here and why are you interested in Bill Duckett and why are you dragging me into it?"

He said nothing, but picked up his briefcase, set it on the table, flipped up the lid and shuffled through the pockets until he found what he was looking for; a newspaper clipping preserved in transparent laminate.

Taken from the Birmingham Evening Mail, it was a year old and headed by a photograph of the young woman the article concerned. Beneath the picture was a report on her death. While on holiday in Fuengirola, Yolande Kalinsky was found murdered in a remote barn, several miles inland. She was naked, hanged by her ankles, and her throat had been cut.

I shuddered at the frightening images the tale thrust into my mind. That poor girl. What torment had she endured before expiring?

Putting aside my revulsion, the name stuck an instant bell. I looked up and at Nathan. "A family member?"

He was struggling to contain his emotions. "My daughter."

Like oil finding its way to the surface of the ocean, the truth began to emerge from the lies he had given me over the last few days. He told me he was divorced and that was true. Yet he lived in York, and the report was from a Birmingham newspaper, so it was a safe bet that his daughter, if not his ex-wife, had moved to the West Midlands.

I took a breath and passed the clipping back to him. "Tell me."

"It's a long story and I don't know if I can hold myself together long enough. But do you have time?"

"Dennis will probably call me at some point, but I'm listening. What brought you here?"

"The remote connection between Fay Selkirk and Bill Duckett...as I already told you."

He looked towards the conservatory, but I felt he was trying to see out of the house and other than the small, side window behind him, he couldn't. Even then it was only a view of the pebbledash garage wall. I suspected the sparkle of tears in his eye and he was trying, once again, to control himself.

He came back to me, cradled his beaker, and went into the tale. "I met my wife when I was stationed near Stafford. When we split up, she took Yolande and moved back to the Midlands. Not much love lost between Anne and me, but I doted on my daughter and I made the journey down there whenever I could. Despite her parents breaking up, Yolande grew up smart, independent, clever and well-adjusted. She was aged twenty-three last year when she went to Costa del Sol with a group of girls from the offices where she worked. They all came back. Yolande didn't... well, she did, but in a body bag. Can you imagine how I felt, Chrissy?"

I thought of Dennis. "Some," I agreed.

"When Anne first rang and told me, I jumped on a plane to Malaga, and met with the local police. They had nothing. That's not a criticism. Don't take any notice of the things you might read in the tabloids. Those guys are every bit as good as ours, but they had next to no forensic from the crime scene. Semen, from which they got DNA, fingerprints of course, but the killer, whoever he was, was not on any database. Her friends said she was in a bar with them. She went to the ladies and never came back. They guessed she'd latched onto some man, but they didn't know who. That was it. That was all the Spanish police could tell me, and when I contacted Yolande's friends personally, they couldn't add anything. They were the ones who raised the alarm when Yolande didn't show the next day. She had been hanging like a piece of meat in that damned barn for forty-eight hours when they found her."

I sensed his anger beginning to rise, and I could understand it. How would I feel if it had been Simon or Ingrid? I recalled the night of The Incident and my fury when the initial distress faded, the way I had attacked the prime suspect the following day. Examining myself further, I found it curious how I'd been ready to tear him apart ten minutes ago, and now, my silent sympathy was going out to him.

He took a deep breath and a large gulp of tea to calm down. "I'm a private eye. What do I do? I ask questions. So I asked questions... and got no answers. Then, early this year, I was working for a warehousing firm at Wetherby. Thefts. They called me in to finger the culprit or culprits. Once I had them, they would deal with the matter. I happened to be in the security office, monitoring the internal CCTV, when I heard two women talking about a novel they had read. But, of course, it wasn't *Crushed*. It was *Exsanguination*, by Anita Stocker. These two girls were mad fans of Anita's, and they were talking about the way the victim was raped then hanged by her ankles, her throat slashed open and left to bleed to death."

"And that brought it all back to you."

"It did more than that, Chrissy. I bought the book and read it. The circumstances of the victim's murder were exactly the same as my daughter's. Stocker even named the victim Yolande and the crime took place on the Costa del Sol. You know what our game is all about. You start with a suspicion, and it won't let go, so you dig deeper into it. I began to read Stocker's books. I started with *Crushed*, her very first novel. The one I told you about, the one she told you about. I did more than read them. I researched real crimes that matched those in the books, and that's when I turned up the tale of Bill Duckett's demise. I did it again with her other books, and time and again, I came across the same situation, but in every case, including that of my daughter, the murder was committed a month or two before the books came out. I checked everything she wrote, and out of thirty-five or six novels, I found ten matches in real life. I didn't believe she was basing her works on those crimes because she could never write them that fast. She – or someone close to her – was writing the books, then committing the crimes to ensure the descriptions were accurate."

I cut in on him. "I'm sorry, but that's not true. According to legend, Georges Simenon could write a novel in as little as two weeks."

"Yes. I know. And that's what stopped me taking any further action. Until this week."

"Fay Selkirk?"

"Exactly. The murder hit the headlines, Anita was taken in for questioning a matter of hours later, but I'd already made the connection. A vicious murder in Haxford, Anita Stocker lived in Haxford. I'll leave you to work out who tipped the police off."

It didn't take much effort. "You?"

He nodded. "She was the catalyst in all these cases, and I didn't know for sure that she would use Fay's death in one of her books, but it was a strong favourite, and I was right. When they let her go, I guessed it was time for me to show up in Haxford."

I could not fault his reasoning, but I still had bones of contention which I needed clarified. "Why didn't you tell me all this when you first arrived? Why the cover story of working for WDIG?"

"It wasn't really intended for you. It was more for the benefit of the police. If I turned up and announced myself as Nathan Kalinsky, they might have made the connection between me and Yolande. So I came up with a cover story, pretending to be interested in the murder of Bill Duckett, which of course, they still maintain was an accident. Just about everything else is true, Chrissy. Quinn gave me short shrift and told me if I wanted to know about Bill Duckett, I should speak to Dennis. I could understand his point of view. Remember, I was a military policeman, and although we didn't get half the flak the civvy police do, I knew that if Bill Duckett's death turned out to be murder, Quinn's backside would be on the line. He was SIO in the case. From what you've told me, I guess you don't like Paddy, but the general word is that he has a good track record and he doesn't deserve that."

"I wouldn't say I don't like him. He's been quite supportive since The Incident. I just find him a bit gung-ho."

"And I'd agree. As it happens, he did me a huge favour when he sent me after Dennis. Obviously, I didn't know he was taking the mick, and I've made my feelings plain on the matter, which is where I was this morning when you couldn't get me at the hotel. But I have to say, it turned out a godsend because it introduced me to you and if you hadn't been with me these last few days, I'd be nowhere."

I appreciated the compliment but it served to remind me of the previous day and that brought my anger to the surface again. "And I suppose it was all a part of your overall plan to guarantee my assistance by giving me a good seeing to on the moors?"

He held up his hand, palms out. "Hell, no." His protest sounded convincing, but then, so had his performance as Nathan Evanson. "I've been telling you since we first met that you're a damned attractive woman, Chrissy. Yesterday was all about me and you, not Anita Stocker, not Bill Duckett, not

Yolande. You and me."

"Even though I'm married." I was beginning to fume again. "I mean, did you think I was hard up for it or something?"

His smile was almost apologetic. "Nothing of the kind. I'll repeat it until the cows come home if have to. You're a good looking woman, the kind of woman a man like me – unattached coming into his middle years – is naturally attracted to."

A memory flashed into my mind. "Do you mean a MILF?" I didn't know what the term MILF meant. It was something Simon had said the day after The Incident when I answered the door to him while I was wearing little else but a transparent nightie. When Simon wouldn't explain it, I realised it was to do with the naughtier side of life, but that was all I knew.

Nathan frowned. "That's not a very nice description of any woman, and it's not how I see you."

I tutted. "I wish someone would tell me what it means."

He laughed. "You mean you don't know?"

"I wouldn't be asking if I did."

"It's not very complimentary, Chrissy."

"Just tell me or it'll drive me round the bend. I've been trying to work it out since my son first said it." That wasn't true. In fact I'd forgotten all about it until Nathan passed his flattering comments a few moments ago.

He gaped. "Your son called you a MILF?"

"Well, no. It didn't happen like that. He was… never mind how it came about, just tell me what it stands for."

"You could look it up online, you know."

Of course I could, but it was such a trivial event with Simon that I'd never thought about it. "Nathan, tell me."

So he did. His cheeks were burning when he spelled it out. Mine were on fire when he was through translating.

"Wait while I see that son of mine again." In order to overcome the embarrassment, I moved the subject sideways. "What about the bull plop you gave me about making sure I was paid when WDIG recoup their losses?"

"It's not all bull. All right, so I wasn't really working for them, but if we can demonstrate that Anita Stocker murdered her husband, they will reclaim the money, and trust me, Chrissy, I'm used to negotiating with big companies like them. I'll secure us a percentage and I'll make sure you get half of that."

"And if it's not Anita?"

"Then she will pay you when we unmask the killer. Either way, you won't lose."

I was just about mollified. "And talking of Anita, you seriously believe she's mixed up in these murders, don't you?"

He shrugged. "It's difficult to come to any other conclusion, and you suspected it too. I suppose it could be a fan, like the women in the warehouse office who first put me onto it, but how do we explain the way the murders happened so soon before the books came out? Trust me, I checked this every which way from Sunday. She self-publishes, so in every case we know the exact date of publication, and in nine of the ten cases, the murders happened a matter of weeks before the books were released. The only exception is Fay Selkirk, but that's because *Utter Carnage* isn't out yet." He paused to take another drink. "I'm not saying she is the perpetrator, but she must know more than she's letting on."

Chapter Fifteen

I was finding it difficult to take all this in. "These ten murders. Were they spread evenly over the ten years?"

"To a point. Odd years there have been two, other years none, but it averages out at one per year."

"And aside from your daughter, were they all in the Haxford area?" I asked the question for two reasons. One, because I felt sure that if they had been in and around Haxford we'd have heard a lot more about it, and two, because I knew of one – two if I counted Yolande Kalinsky – which happened nowhere near Haxford.

He soon put me right. "No. In fact the only two in this area are Bill Duckett and Fay Selkirk. Ten years between them, which is why there's been no connection made by the media. The others happened all over the country, my daughter in southern Spain. I'm surprised that no one put it together before I did. Maybe they did. There are plenty of geeks out there who come up with conspiracy theories on this kind of stuff, and remember, I only put it together because of a chance remark from a couple of warehouse security women."

"You mean security officers."

"My bad."

Logic began to seep through my tumultuous emotions. "You're going to have to demonstrate that Anita was in the area where and when each of these murders was committed."

"You mean *we'll* have to demonstrate that. Yes, you're right. We know for a fact that she and Sebastian were on the Costa del Sol at the time of Yolande's murder, and they were both in Haxford when Bill was killed and Fay, but that's all we know."

I was beginning to suffer information overload. I finished my tea. "If you'll excuse me for one minute, I'll check on Dennis."

It was an excuse. If Dennis had been awake he would have buzzed me, but he hadn't, and when I popped my head in through the bedroom door, he was still sleeping. I could see streaks down his cheeks where he had probably been crying. The only times in his life I'd ever seen him cry was at the birth of our two children – tears of joy – and after his father's death – grief. If I was having a torrid time dealing with his condition, I was not alone. He was having it just as bad if not worse.

Yet I was glad he was still resting because what I really needed was a few minutes to myself, away from Nathan, away from Dennis, away from the pressure, and it had nothing to do with the case. It was all about me. I had to sort out the raging confusion of emotions bubbling away inside like a cauldron. I sat in the toilet, my head pounding under an avalanche of mental images and counterpoints and contradictions from the last twenty-four hours.

Counterpoint? Contradiction? Is that what it was called when some man tries to get your frillies off, and you're tempted, and then change your mind, and then confess to your daughter-in-law because... Because why? Because I stopped him? Because deep down, I really wanted him? Because I couldn't betray Dennis?

My attitude to Nathan had undergone a double about face in the space of the last hour, switching from my initial attraction, to the fury of suspected betrayal, to sympathetic resonance in the face of someone who had known appalling violence to a family member. I guessed that his suffering was far worse than mine, and I dare not ask how he (and his ex-wife) had coped with it. I had enough problems trying to deal with my troubles without taking his on board, and I still had my husband, but thoughts of Yolande's terrible demise served only to prompt memories of the previous day's incident out on the moors. Had I known then what I knew about him now would I have yielded, let him have his way, let him sublimate his grief, his agony, in sexual gratification? It was an imponderable, one of those theoretical exercises to which I would never know the answer because it didn't happen and would never happen, but before I stopped him the previous day, the very same notion, sublimation to combat stress, was probably at work somewhere deep in the back of my mind.

'Did you think I was hard up for it?' That was the question I'd asked him less than twenty minutes ago. Now I turned it on its head. Was he hard up for it? Doubtful. Such a good looking man surely would have no problem securing dates, and some of those dates would inevitably end up putting a strain on the mattress or flattening moorland grass. Alternatively, did he, like me, see it as a means of distracting him from the terrible anguish he must be suffering at the thought of Yolande's horrific end? If that was so, what was I to make of his serial compliments? *'You're a damned attractive woman, Chrissy.'* *'The kind of woman a man like me – unattached coming into his middle years – is naturally attracted to.'* *'(MILF) is not a very nice description of any woman, and it's not how I see you.'* Were they nothing more than hot air, a means to get me laid under him so he could immerse his whole being in the conjunction of our bodies, help him forget, if only for a few minutes?

Stood at the basin, washing my hands, I looked into Dennis's shaving mirror and mentally asked that reflection, "Who am I looking at?" As Nathan was so fond of telling me, I felt I was a good looking woman. Certainly not a fifty-three-year-old hag, never a man-hunting vamp, but not a classic beauty either. An ordinary, everyday woman, better looking than some, not as alluring as others.

'You should have let him. It would do you no end of good.' The core message of Naomi's words rang round my head, and looking in that mirror, I could see a woman who certainly needed something to give her a lift, something to help clear the bags under those eyes, put some sparkle, some colour in those cheeks, bring a smile to those lips. But a rampant half hour with another man?

Five weeks. Five short weeks. That was how long it had taken for this breezy woman, one who actively looked on the brighter side of life, to sink into an ever-deepening pit of despair.

What to do about it?

I don't know that Dennis had ever faced such confusion, but I do know how he would handle it. He was not a bad-tempered man. In thirty years, I'd never even heard him swear like other men do. When he was on the point of losing it, he would vent his frustration on the job around him: take it out on the engine, hit the exhaust with a bigger hammer, rev the engine, faster, harder than normal, and eventually, the irritation, the annoyance, would settle, go away.

I didn't deal with inanimate objects. My work set me against recalcitrant people, and as that thought came to me, I reached a decision. What better way to deal with my current frustrations than confront one of the most obdurate and arrogant women it had ever been my misfortune to encounter: Anita, enviably gorgeous, Stocker.

I don't know how long I was gone, but when I returned to the kitchen, it was to find Nathan chatting with Naomi, and for the second time, I thought about her opinion of the previous afternoon. *'You should have let him.'*

If the position had been reversed, if she were caring for Simon after a major incident and some man like Nathan made advances, would she yield? My guess was yes. Not that she did not love Simon, but she would have no hesitation in seeking such release from the pressure as she could get.

Curiously, I could not find it within myself to condemn her for such an attitude, if indeed it was her attitude, and my refusal to sit in judgement came from personal experience of the devastation wreaked by mindless violence.

"Hi, Chrissy," she greeted me. "Bethany's in preschool, and I've a couple of hours to spare. I figured you and Nathan might want to chase up your case. I can stick it out until, say, quarter past two, when I'll have to go pick madam up."

I looked at Nathan. "Would it be a good idea to see Anita again?"

He smiled. "The best suggestion you've made all morning."

"An hour," I said to Naomi. "Ninety minutes at the most."

"That's cool."

Minutes later, frying in the morning heat, we climbed into Nathan's VW, he started the engine and we pulled out, along the street and onto Moor Road.

"You were gone a long time," he observed. "Dennis needed some serious attention did he?"

"What? Oh, no. He was spark out. I, er, I needed the smallest room."

"Ah."

We began the steep descent into Haxford and he held the car back on the brakes.

"Nathan. About yesterday—"

"My fault entirely, dear lady. I thought you were… what's a polite way of putting it?"

"Easy?"

"Good lord, no." His shock sounded genuine. "I

was thinking more, er, approachable, amenable, up for it, although that last does sound a bit uncomplimentary."

"I'm sorry. Not sorry that I stopped you, and it's not because I don't find you attractive. I do. And even at my age, I can be quite lively. I'm not a lie on your back and check whether the ceiling needs a coat of paint woman. But I am an old-fashioned faithful wife. I don't do that kind of thing."

"We can go on all day apologising to one another. Let's just chalk it down to the realms of an unfortunate error on my part, and put it behind us. You have my assurance that it won't happen again."

That was better, only now I didn't know whether to feel happy or disappointed. It cleared the air between us, consigned the unfortunate, brief but exciting incident to history, but the confusion, which was still there, boggling my tired mind, left me a little miffed that he wouldn't try again. Maybe next time…

He cut me off. "Why were you trying to contact me this morning?"

I hardly heard what he said. "What? I'm sorry, I wasn't listening."

"You said you rang WDIG which is how you knew I had nothing to do with them. What was it you wanted when you couldn't find me?"

"It's probably irrelevant now since you've already checked up on Anita's books, but I was at the supermarket this morning and I picked up a copy of one of her novels from the charity table. *Squelched*, it's called, and there were two victims dropped alive into—"

"A pulping machine in a paper factory. Yes. I already know about it. The reality happened somewhere on the outskirts of Manchester about five years ago. It's unsolved and they were murdered on page ten of the book. Am I right?"

"On the button."

As he drove, he dipped into his pocket. "While I think on, I have something for you. I have it stored on my laptop, but I printed a copy for you."

He handed me a single, badly folded sheet of A4 on which was printed a list of words.

Crushed
Butchery
Decapitation
Exterminated
Torture unto death
Squelched
Termination
Knifeman
Exsanguination
Utter carnage

They might have meant nothing, but I recognised *Crushed, Squelched*, and *Utter Carnage* as titles of Anita's books, and I guessed the rest. "These are the books which matched real life murders?"

"Yes. And they're in the order they were published. If you think it'll help, I can give you the publication dates, but they didn't really do me any favours."

"And I don't think they'll mean much to me either. You've already done the research and highlighted the proximity of the murders to the publication dates."

"So how do you propose we go ahead, facing Anita Stocker this morning?"

"Give it to her." I gave him a naughty smile. "The way I wouldn't let you give it to me yesterday."

Nathan laughed, and for the first time since the previous afternoon, I felt some of the amity between us returning.

"Are you going to stand by with a video camera?"

Now, I chuckled. "It would make an interesting vlog, wouldn't it, but would it stand up in court? Not confession under duress but confession under seduction?"

He laughed again. "You know, I'd love to have met you before this business with Dennis.

"No you wouldn't. If I wasn't so stressed out by Dennis's injuries, I'd have left you with a few bruises yesterday afternoon." I sighed. "I'm an optimist, Nathan, but since The Incident, whatever faith I had in the future has taken a good kicking. Maybe I need a good kicking to get it back."

Keeping his right hand on the wheel, he reached across with his left and took my hand. "You'll get there. Strong women like you always do. It's something to do with your northern heritage."

"What do you mean my northern heritage? You're from the North, aren't you? Or has someone moved York to somewhere south of the M5?"

"I come from Peterborough originally. I'm based in York now, but that's because I was at Turnhill when I came out of the army, and I'd been there for some time. I liked the area, liked the people, so I decided to make it my home. Face it, there's nothing for me anywhere else."

We were climbing the twisty, winding lane up to Hilly Farm, and as we levelled out on the plateau and passed the rough layby, yesterday's episode came back to haunt me briefly. I buried it and forced thoughts of the confrontation to come. Anita Stocker would not like what we had to say, but the past twenty-four hours had robbed me of any empathy for her. And that was an unusual situation for me. The woman was a widow, and that alone was usually enough to engender my sympathies. Her wealth, her classy figure, good looks, meant little or nothing to me. All right, so I was a bit peeved by her figure and her appearance and the expensive clothes she wore to lounge around on her equally expensive furniture, but I guessed it was all a consequence of her wealth, and it would have been interesting to meet her when she was plain old Janet Duckett. All that aside, she did not deserve to be left alone, bringing up an arrogant and narcissistic son by herself at such an age. She should have had a least another fifteen, perhaps twenty years with Bill.

That, however, was no excuse for this list of crimes, and she had some explaining to do.

As Nathan pulled in behind her Range Rover, I noticed that the Volvo saloon, which I assumed was Sebastian's, was missing. Pity. I would love to shove all this in his face, too.

As we climbed out, I also noticed that the front door was open. We exchanged cautious glances, and Nathan rang the bell. No answer. He pushed the door, and we made our tentative way inside, turning automatically into the front room.

The first thing that really took my eye was a laptop on the coffee table, lid raised, screen active, a word processed document, staring out at us, the cursor flashing at the end of the single line of type as if waiting for more input.

And then I looked at her, sat in her favourite chair by the fireside, shapely legs extended (typical) arms fallen to her lap … her face a ghostly pale, and a kitchen knife, its blade covered in blood, sunk into her abdomen just beneath her breastbone.

Chapter Sixteen

Nathan took out his phone and was about to dial 999 but I overcame my initial shock and stopped him. "Let me ring Mandy direct. It'll be quicker than waiting for the emergency operators to get onto the local station."

He nodded and disappeared into the kitchen while I made the call and told Mandy what we had found.

"Stay where you are, Chrissy, and don't go wandering around the house. You of all people should know the script. Don't touch anything. Are you sure she's dead?"

"Bearing in mind, you've just told me not to touch anything, I'm working from her appearance only, but it looks as if she's been dead for a while. Oh, and while I think on, there's no sign of Sebastian and his car is missing. He's probably in Haxford somewhere. Try a few furniture shops or hairdressers; anywhere where there are plenty of mirrors."

"I'll get uniforms out looking for him. You stay put and we'll be with you in twenty minutes."

"You've got it."

Nathan returned from the kitchen wearing a pair of washing-up gloves, which looked too tight for his hands.

"What are you doing?" I asked.

He held up a memory stick. "I'm going to take a quick look at her laptop, find the documents folder, and download the contents onto this."

"Nathan, Mandy's just asked us not to touch anything."

"Which is why I'm wearing the marigolds. What? Did you think I was going to wash up a few pots while we waited for the police? I won't be touching the keyboard, only the mouse pad and buttons."

"Yes, but Anita's fingerprints will be all over those, and you'll mess them up. Paddy Quinn will have a screaming fit when he finds out."

"If he finds out." Nathan made himself comfortable on the settee, inserted the memory stick into a USB port, shuffled through a few menus and right-clicked the documents folder. He checked the properties. "You see. Less than two gigabytes. It'll only take a minute to copy it all onto this." He surfed a few menus, and I watched the relevant screens appear and detail the progress of the procedure. In fact, it took almost ten minutes and I was getting anxious, worrying that the police would arrive before the task was complete. But then it was done. He removed the memory stick, dropped it in his pocket, and then took the marigolds back to the kitchen. "We can have a look at that at our leisure later on." He gave me a smile which I think was supposed to encourage me. "Come on, Chrissy. We need to bend the rules now and then. I mean, you hired that…" He trailed off and a frown crossed his brow. "And talking of that muppet, why haven't we heard from Myner, the guy you hired to hack Anita's system?"

I called upon my hazy memory of the last couple of days. "I had one message from him telling me he had got into Anita's system, and that's the last I heard of him."

"In that case, we'll have to speak to Lester Grimes again, see if we can get in touch with the mynah bird."

Silence prevailed for a few minutes, and barely able to comprehend the shocking discovery, it was me who broke it. "Why did she do it? Why suicide?"

"I think we may be responsible, Chrissy. Yesterday, we confronted her with our suspicions, and she knew that we were close to the truth and it was only a matter of time before we got there. Have you read the screen?"

"Well, no. I'm not really into her novels. Not even the opening lines."

"It's nothing to do with a novel. Have a read."

I perched on the settee next to him, and read the single line of text.

This can't go on. It has to end here. I should of done it sooner.

"As good as a confession, if you want my opinion," Nathan said. "She carried out the murders. Some bizarre notion of research, I suppose, finding out what happens when you kill people using such brutal methods so she could describe them accurately in her books."

It would, I thought, be entirely in keeping with

Anita Stocker. From the brief time I'd spent in her company, I realised that the only thing of any importance in her life was her. The people she had murdered, including her husband, the poor couple I had read about in *Squelched* (what an appalling title) and Nathan's daughter, would have meant nothing to her. They were as rats in a laboratory, useful for experimental purposes only.

A quarter of an hour later, several cars, their blue lights and headlamps flashing in the afternoon sun, pulled along the track and stopped, hemming in both the Range Rover and Nathan's VW.

With everyone but Nathan and me clad in forensic suits, Paddy Quinn came hurtling in with all the speed of an SAS commando, followed at a more leisurely pace by Mandy, and behind her were my son, Simon, and a small team of uniforms.

I collared Simon immediately. "Naomi's with your father, and she's expecting me back. We're not going to make it, Simon. Give her a bell, tell her to ask Mrs McQuarrie if she'll sit in until Paddy and Mandy are finished with us."

"Already done, Mam. I guessed she'd be at yours and I rang while we were on our way out here. Nam says it's no problem. She'll get old Ma McQ in."

"Her name is Naomi, and old Ma McQ is Mrs McQuarrie to you."

He ignored my protest. "Are you all right?"

I nodded. "Yes. I'm fine."

"It's just that with all this coming on top of Dad—"

I stopped him. "I said I'm all right, Simon. As long as someone is with your father, I'll be fine.

Now stop worrying about me and get on with your job."

Paddy and Mandy had made their initial examination, and the inspector turned angry eyes on Nathan and me. "What are you two doing here? You, Evanson, are a pain in the backside. I told you to clear off the other day. And I'm surprised at you, Christine. Haven't you got enough on your plate looking after Dennis?"

"Yes, Paddy, I have, but I've also got the problem of looking after our income and where it's going to come from. Anita was a paying client." I purposely avoided looking at the dead woman and waved an arm in her vague direction. "It doesn't look like I'll get paid now, does it? I'll have to make a claim against her estate."

He was appalled. "She's dead, for God's sake."

I sighed. "I had realised that, but I'm doing what everyone else in this world seems to do. Prioritising me first." I did not mean it. I only said it to irritate Paddy. Standing off to one side, from the way she winked at me, I guessed Mandy realised as much.

"What are you doing here anyway?" It was Quinn, pushing again.

I was about to remind him that I'd just said Anita was my client, but Nathan got in first. "We're chasing up a lead, Inspector. Christine and I are both private eyes, and that's what we do."

"What lead?"

"The link between Anita Stocker's novels and real-life murders."

Paddy fumed, and I knew that any moment now he would explode. "That? Again? I told you about

Bill Duckett the other day. It was an accident."

Nathan would probably have taken him on, but I stepped in to pour oil on troubled waters. "We had our doubts, Paddy. That's all."

Quinn rounded on one of his uniforms. "You, get statements from these two." He came back to us. "When you've given your statement, get in your car and clear off. The both of you. I don't wanna see you round here again."

"One thing, Paddy," I insisted.

"What?"

"All your cars are blocking us in."

A good twenty minutes passed before we eventually climbed into Nathan's car, and one of the uniforms cleared the way, so we could reverse back along the track, and eventually turn the VW round, and make for the road.

"Why did you stop me?" Nathan asked. "I was about to tell him everything we discovered."

"Trust my judgement, Nathan. I've known Paddy for thirty odd years. Whatever you have to say, he wouldn't listen, and we'd have been there for another couple of hours playing table tennis with theories and counter theories, accusations and dismissals. It's better if we just go our own sweet way, and then when we've solved everything, we can present him with a fait accompli. Even then, we won't get any credit. Once he's made the arrest, he'll claim that the idea was his."

Nathan laughed. "I bow to your superior local knowledge." The layby was coming up on the right. "Are you sure you don't want me to stop, so you can give me the benefit of your greater experience in other areas?"

The remark did not annoy me. If anything it did exactly the opposite. We had reached that stage where we could forget about the previous day's short interlude and joke about it. "Take it from me, you couldn't cope with a woman of my experience." I pointed straight ahead. "Drive on."

I honed my concentration, took out my phone and rang Lester.

"It's the Chrissy I'd love to curl up with. What can I do you for, lass?"

"You can get in touch with Mr Myner for me," I replied. "I was supposed to hear from him, Lester, and I haven't heard anything other than a message to tell me he was on with the job."

"He's like that, luv. Vague. I'd give him another day or two if I were you."

"Not good enough, Lester. Things are hotting up. Tell me where I can find him."

"Well, I don't know. I mean—"

"Lester." My voice carried a warning edge.

"All right, so he lives on Batley Road Estate. Thirty-nine, Trafalgar Avenue, but if he kicks off it's your fault."

"I think I'll be doing the kicking." I ended the call, accessed the online maps, and in seconds, I had isolated Trafalgar Avenue. "When you get to the town centre, Nathan, cut round the northern bypass and I'll direct you from there. It's not far."

His eyes narrowed, concentrating on the road ahead, he said, "You've obviously got something on your mind."

"Anita. It wasn't suicide."

The car wobbled and he took control again. "What? But the note—"

"It's a set up. She was murdered and the killer's trying to make us think she took her own life. Stop thinking like a private eye for a minute, and think like a woman."

"Difficult. I'm a man, as I would like to have proved yesterday."

I tutted. "I thought we were forgetting about yesterday." I paused to calm down. "When committing suicide, most women – men, too, come to that – would cut their wrists. Jamming a large knife into her belly would hurt. She would be in agony until she lost consciousness. We both know that she was vain and selfish. Even if she had reached the end of her tether, she'd have been more likely to use pills, but if she had to resort to cold steel, it would have been her wrists."

He was silent for a little while, negotiating the bends, keeping his speed down to cope with the steep descent. He reached a straight stretch of road before he responded.

"You know, not only are you a cracking looking woman, but you're also a clever private detective. It takes a special kind of investigative mind to put such slender threads together, and now that you've pointed it out, you're absolutely right. The dress she was wearing must have cost a fortune, and given her vanity, she probably wouldn't want to mess it up, let alone punch a hole in it. Once again, I am beholden to your superior intellect, Chrissy."

"And so you should be," I said feeling a little more cheerful. I never went out of my way to seek compliments, but Nathan knew how to lay it on thick. Unless he was still hankering after my nether regions. I thought about warning him off, but changed my mind. I could handle the compliments, and if he tried his luck again, I could handle him. "There's more. Did you notice the bruising on her wrists?"

"Oh, that's probably from yesterday."

It was my turn to be surprised. "Huh?"

"If you remember, she was battering me about the chest. I took her wrists and made her sit down."

"Ah. Yes I remember. All the same, I stand by my theory that she didn't commit suicide." I excused myself and rang Naomi, but as Simon had promised, there was no problem.

"It's all right, Chrissy," she reported before I could say a word. "Simon rang me, told me what was going off, and I called Mrs McQuarrie in. She's with Dennis until I get back with Bethany."

"And is he all right? Dennis, I mean?"

"Same as. He looked a little depressed this morning. Part and parcel of his problems, I shouldn't wonder. He kept muttering something about a keep and potent pie. I couldn't make head nor tail of what he was trying to say."

I giggled. "Meat and potato pie. On the day of The Incident, I cooked him one for his tea, and he was seriously looking forward to it. He never did get it. Cappy the Cat dealt with some of it, and I threw the rest away."

Satisfied that my husband was being taken care of, I guided Nathan round the town centre, and onto Batley Road. A quarter of a mile along there, we turned into Mafeking Avenue, the main thoroughfare through the council estate where all the streets were named after famous battles. I pointed the way through a few streets, and onto Trafalgar Avenue.

Number thirty-nine was a ground floor flat in what was a four-storey block. When we buzzed the entry call, we got no answer. Nathan shuffled along the ground floor, peering into the windows. On two occasions, someone came to the window indicated that he should clear off. From the tiny bit I heard, 'clear off' was a cleaned up version of the actual dialogue. At a third window, some man opened the window and told him exactly where he could go, and this time there was no mistaking the Anglo-Saxon.

At the fourth attempt, he stared in, then recoiled, his face spelling out shock.

"We need the cops again."

My heart sank. "Not Myner too?"

"I don't know whether he's dead or alive, but he's spark out, face down on the floor. We need an ambulance and we need the police."

Chapter Seventeen

Getting on for twenty minutes later, Sergeant Vic Hillman turned up, fathomed a way into the block, and when they got to the door of Myner's flat, they had to break in. Nathan and I waited in the lobby, making an effort to reassure the other tenants who came out to see what was going on, and I could imagine the headlines in the Haxford Recorder. By the time the Chinese whispers reached the editor's desk, the police would have been involved in a major raid.

It didn't take long for Vic to come back out again, his phone glued to his ear. "You'd better send the paramedics in, as well," he was saying. "We don't know how long this guy's been unconscious." He listened to the feedback, then finished the call, and concentrated on us.

"I don't wanna hassle you, Chrissy, not while Dennis is the way he is, but what are you doing here?"

"It's linked to that business up at Hilly Farm, Vic. Paddy, Mandy, my Simon, are all up there now, and we needed to talk to Myner."

His face turned to a mask of disapproval. "What are you doing mixing it with lowlife like him? He's a porn merchant. And a hacker. He's got more form than today's racing pages."

"Yes, we know all about him. We asked him to do a favour on behalf of a client."

Hillman shook his head. "I'm surprised at you. I really am. I'm gonna need a statement, and the name of the client so he or she can confirm what you're telling me."

"That's gonna be difficult, Vic. The client is at Hilly Farm with a knife in her belly."

He clenched and unclenched his fists and made a determined effort not to lose his temper. "I've said it before, why don't you just stop at home and look after Dennis? Don't you think you've got enough on—"

I cut him off. "Paddy Quinn said the same, and I don't want to get into the debate with you. Anita Stocker was a client, there was a suspicion her system had been hacked, we asked Myner to check it out for us. He didn't get back to us, so we came here looking for him, Nathan looked through the window, saw him, and I called you guys. That's all there is to it."

He turned to go back into the flat. "I'll get someone to take your statement. After that, you can go home, and I mean go home, Chrissy, not go looking for more trouble."

The journey back to Bracken Close passed in near silence, pretty much like the previous day, but this time it was an anxious quiet, not confused or mistrustful. Nathan concentrated on his driving and I tossed and turned the shocking events of the day over in my mind.

"You'll have to see to Dennis," he said when he

stopped at the end of the drive. "So I'll catch you—
"

I interrupted. "One thing. If you can spare a few minutes, could you copy Anita's documents from that memory stick to my laptop?"

"Yeah. Sure. Why not?"

I grinned. "Thanks. You'll get a cup of tea for your trouble and if you're really good, you might even get a custard cream to go with it."

"But nothing more exciting?"

"If you're lucky, I might have some cake left over from last weekend. It could be a bit stale, but it should still be serviceable." I laughed. "Like me."

He chuckled along with me. "You don't half know how to tempt a man."

We both kept our part of the bargain. He copied Anita's files to my machine and I provided him with tea, biscuits and a piece of madeira cake. Not only him, but everyone else as I discovered when I stepped out onto the rear decking and found not only Mrs McQuarrie, but Naomi and Bethany still in residence. The only person who didn't get cake was me. There wasn't enough, and the single piece I had left was for Dennis. We sat outside for a time, chatting with Mrs McQuarrie and Naomi while Bethany, after wolfing down her piece of cake, hit the sun lounger to sleep off the exertions of preschool. Quite where Cappy the Cat had got to, I don't know and didn't ask.

Dennis put in an appearance at just turned five o'clock, and for a moment I wondered who'd got him out of bed and into the wheelchair and then I remembered that he'd done the same thing at least once during the morning. I was a little concerned when he aimed the chair down the first ramp, from the door to the decking, and I got up to help, but he waved me away, and as if to demonstrate that I need not worry, he held it back using the strength of his hands and arms to keep it under control, and it dawned on me that he really was getting better. He had a long way to go before he could live without the chair, but the signs were there.

I greeted him with a peck on the cheek and went back inside to make him a cup of tea. When I got back, Nathan was telling the two women of our day, and I noticed Dennis giving him a curled lip, sour eye. I don't think my husband liked my new friend very much, and that was so unlike Dennis. Under normal circumstances, he never took for or against another person, male or female, until he knew them better. Perhaps it was because Nathan was fit, strong, in prime of good health, while Dennis was still wheelchair bound, at least for the time being. Or maybe it was because he felt Nathan was stealing my thunder, but that was unlikely. Dennis had always objected to my efforts as a private investigator; poking my nose in, as he described it. According to him we didn't need the money (but we did now) and there was always an element of danger, and I suppose that after the way he was beaten up, there was more than a grain of truth in that. He was left in this state as an indirect consequence of one of my investigations. In other words, if I had not been involved in the case, he would not have been attacked.

Mrs McQuarrie was first to leave, and then

Nathan made his excuses, saying he had work he needed to get on with, and I accompanied him to the front door.

"What is this work?" I asked as he tossed his briefcase into the well of the passenger seat.

"A report for WDIG. I told you, Chrissy, when this comes out, they'll make an effort to reclaim some of the monies paid to Anita when Bill died, and even though they didn't commission us to look into it, I may be able to get us a cut of that money."

"But we haven't proved that Anita did it, and I told you, I don't believe she committed suicide."

"Granted, but if not her, then who? There's only one other candidate, isn't there?"

"Sebastian," I said with a sinking heart.

"Correct, and it could be considered as murdered by a family member in order to cash in on the insurance. It's a hazy area, and it may all come to nothing, but that shouldn't stop us trying." His charm shone through a familiar smile. "Cheer up. You could be in for a healthy payday."

I watched him drive away, then returned to the rear decking where Naomi was on the phone to Simon.

"He's out at Hilly Farm and it's gonna be another late one," she said when the call ended. "I'd better get missy home and sort out some tea for us."

"Why not stay here," I suggested. "It'd be nice for us to have a bit of company for tea, wouldn't it, Dennis?"

He grunted and Naomi protested. "I don't want to put on you."

"Don't be daft. It's no problem."

She gave way. "All right, but only if you let me help in the kitchen."

She didn't because I rang for pizza, but she and Bethany did stay with Dennis until everything was ready, and we passed a pleasant evening over a simple meal, Bethany chattering away, telling us all about her new friends at preschool, Naomi speculating on return to work in a year or two when her daughter went to school proper, and I felt truly relaxed for the first time in a good while. It was the way I had always envisaged life. A family meal, just like it was when Simon and Ingrid were children.

Naomi went home at seven, and I settled Dennis in front of the television, but he shooed me away when I offered to pick his channels. The signs were there. He was on the mend and could manage the remote for himself.

The ambient feeling of contentment didn't last long. Mandy rang at half past seven.

"You're not going to like this, Chrissy, but Anita Stocker's suicide—"

"Was murder," I interrupted.

She tutted. "I should have known you'd make the connection. Go on, surprise me. How did you guess?"

I spent a few minutes running the same explanation past her that I'd given Nathan.

"Deduction, eh? Christine Sherlock Capper. It makes sense, but that's not what told us. I'm not going to go into any detail, but forensics found indications that there was someone else in the house."

"Sebastian?"

"No. Oh, we found plenty of traces of Seb Stocker, and we do need to question him, but we still think there was another person in the house. We just don't know who yet, and it's all about waiting for forensics to get back to us."

I shifted the subject sideways. "Have you been told about Eddie Myner?"

"Yep. Vic Hillman rang. Myner's alive, but he'll be in dry dock for a while. The big question is, what were you two doing looking for him?"

"Hacking Anita Stocker's system."

"Chrissy, that is illegal."

"So is murder, but when Nathan approached Paddy on the death of Bill Duckett, it didn't seem to matter, even though everything pointed to murder. And while we were all happy to blame Anita for either suggesting or actually committing Fay Selkirk's murder, there was always the possibility that her system had been hacked and someone else had got hold of that manuscript. The same someone who tipped you people off. I was introduced to Eddie, and I paid him to hack the system and tell me whether it had been hacked before. You knew about it. I told you when you were here yesterday."

"Yes, but I didn't think you'd go through with it. Anyway, according to Vic Hillman you'll never find out. Whoever beat Eddie half to death, trashed all his gear. It'll take our techies weeks to put it all back together again, and even then they'll have to go through the entire system to see whether you got it right. On the other hand, the attack on him seems to indicate that you were onto something. It's all up in the air, Chrissy, and our priority now is to try and identify this person who was in the house when Anita was murdered."

"Well, I can tell you that Nathan and I stuck to the living room. And you're not being fair, Mandy, keeping it to yourself. How do you know there was another person there when she was murdered? Come on. This is Chrissy. One of your besties."

She gave way. "Bruising to Anita's neck and wrist."

"I can explain the wrists," I said and gave her an account of Nathan's confrontation with Anita the previous day.

She was grateful but went on, "According to the pathologist, someone else was wielding that knife. He held her by the back of the neck, and she took hold of his hand to try and stop him ramming the knife home. Alternatively, when he jammed the knife in, she made to remove it, and he took hold of her wrist to pull her hand away. You obviously don't think so, but the pathologist will tell us for sure one way or the other. Either way, he bruised her, and it's all down to whatever the path lab can get from those injuries." There was a brief pause. "Let me just repeat what I'm always saying, Chrissy. If you come across anything, anything at all, no matter how tiny, give us a bell. Ring me, not Paddy. He's up to his eyes in it, and Dennis's condition aside, you never were his favourite person."

"You know you can count on me." I changed the subject again. "Sebastian. My money would be on him. Have you found him yet?"

"Nope, and if we assume he's innocent, we don't know whether he's aware that his mother's dead yet. And on that note, I'll have to go."

I'd been so settled in the friendly, family evening, that I'd all but forgotten I was in the middle of a nasty little case, but Mandy's call reminded me, and when she rang off, I made sure Dennis was all right, left him to his repeats of Top Gear, and made my way to my workstation at the rear of the room, where I booted up the machine and then emptied my bag and pockets of the flotsam I had collected during the day. This amounted to a couple of till receipts, but I couldn't remember what I'd actually bought, and a crumpled sheet of A4 paper, which when I opened it, turned out to be the list of Anita Stocker's ten titles, books which had mirrored real life murders, all of which had seen the murder take place on page ten.

It was one of those silly little things which had been there all along, but which neither Nathan nor I paid much attention to. Why did she always choose to murder the victim on page ten? Or was it no more than coincidence? The moment I thought of coincidence, I dismissed it out of hand. Three, four, five titles with the murder on page ten, I would have accepted as coincidence, but not all ten of them. Even so, that did not make it suspicious. Perhaps Anita Stocker had some ingrained superstition regarding the number ten, a similar thing to the way we all regarded thirteen as unlucky. Perhaps it was the opposite with her. Perhaps ten was her lucky number and on that basis, she killed off her fictitious victims on page ten to ensure the books would be successful.

As I looked at the list of titles, a sense of intrigue came over me. I guessed Nathan had written them as he saw them on whatever list he had consulted, because each one began with a capital letter, and not everyone took the trouble to ensure such correct English.

Crushed
Butchery
Decapitation
Exterminated
Squelched
Torture unto death
Termination
Knifeman
Exsanguination
Utter carnage

As I read down the list, those capitals looked almost like some kind of anagram: C, B, D, E, S, T, T, K, E, U. It remained to be seen what kind of words could be derived from the letters, but it was short of useful vowels; two E's and a U. So maybe it was just my tired mind playing games, playing tricks even.

I spent a little time pondering the situation. Sebastian Stocker was still favourite in my eyes, even though Mandy insisted there was someone else in the house. I don't know where they got that from but they usually had good grounds for saying it, and if Paddy insisted Mandy needed to keep it to herself, she would.

But if it was Sebastian, what was his motive? He was a prime example of narcissism in my opinion, and to look at his car, a nearly new Volvo costing anything up to £30,000 on the road, it didn't look as if mummy kept him short of money. If he decided he wanted to see the back of her, it would leave him in financial limbo until such times as her will cleared probate. He wouldn't even be paid the salary Anita told us she paid him. Perhaps that was the rationale behind Paddy and Mandy's thinking, and maybe that's why they insisted it had to be someone else.

Right away, I knew I was wrong. The police did not make assumptions based on a suspect's apparent lack of motive. They would not assume there was someone else in that house just because they didn't think the killer was Sebastian. They had physical evidence – the bruising to her neck and (perhaps) her wrist – and they must have something else. It need not be much. Fibres, a stray, partial fingerprint, just a tiny something the CSI team had come across but enough to expand the range of suspicion.

Looking on the screen of my laptop, I reasoned that it could be something they had found in her files, and I remembered that Nathan had copied them to my machine. Time for my ingrained nosy parker skills to come into play.

Chapter Eighteen

I had plenty of free space on the laptop, which was just as well because the folder named 'stockerdocs' came in at just under two gigabytes and when I checked the properties, it contained over 11,000 files. I opened the folder and to my relief, I learned that everything was organised into folders, the single largest of which was 'books'. When I opened it I found some odd files and each of her novels in its own folder.

There were thirty-seven such folders, which I found odd. I was sure Nathan told me she'd produced only thirty-five books. Or maybe he was generalising.

I doubted that they would tell me anything, and anyway, with her predilection for grotesque slaughter, I didn't fancy checking out thirty-seven page tens. With the memory of her blood-stained body still fresh in my mind, lined up alongside the mindless violence meted out to Eddie Myner, I'd had enough real life brutality for one day.

Pulling out of 'books', I sat back for a moment and asked myself what I was looking for. Answers was the word that sprang immediately to mind, but answers to what? Anita Stocker. That's what. So I ran a search for 'Stocker' and came up with a plethora of hits, most of which were linked to her book files. Then I remembered that her name was not Anita Stocker. It was Janet Duckett. I ran a second search, for 'Duckett' this time, and although I got a lot of results, the name of one folder stood out: 'myab'. Many people used acronyms or contractions for their folder names, and I knew Anita did – look at *uttcar* – and this one intrigued me enough to open it and I struck gold. It was her autobiography. Unfinished, of course, because she didn't live long enough to complete it.

From the very first page, the foreword, I knew that this would open up fresh avenues, perhaps not into investigation of the real-life murders, but into the real Anita Stocker, and the issues which drove her.

My name is Janet Duckett but I'm better known as bestselling novelist, Anita Stocker. I was born and raised in Haxford, West Yorkshire and I had a happy and contented childhood and teenage years. It was only in my early twenties, after I met and married William Duckett, that my life turned into the kind of nightmare many of my fictitious characters would come to suffer.

Skipping the chapters on her early life, I discovered that she met Bill Duckett when she was twenty-one years of age, and he was coming up to his fortieth. She was the same age as me and before I actually read it, I worked out that he was still working for Addison's at the time they met, still teaching Dennis, Tony and Greg their trade.

According to Anita, he was a charming and (as she later learned) virile man. He was also worth quite bit of money, albeit mostly tied up in Hilly Farm. What more could a young woman want than a man who was able to satisfy her and keep her in luxury. It didn't pan out like that. They were married a year after meeting, and a couple of months later, had their first serious row, which ended when he hit her. And it wasn't just a slap. A clenched fist which blacked her eye. She said she was packing and going, and he warned her that the only way she would ever be allowed to leave him was in her coffin. That argument occurred on the 10th of October, the tenth of the tenth.

At that point, I thought I had discovered her problem with the number ten, but I was mistaken. It went much deeper than that, as I learned in the next chapter, *'Ten, My Bête Noir'*.

Despite her early claim to have had a happy childhood, an uncle molested her when she was ten years old. It was the only such incident she mentioned. Her mother, whom she loved, passed away on the tenth day of January a year after Janet became Janet Duckett, her only son, Sebastian, was born in October, the tenth month, a year after Bill Duckett first struck her (there were more such incidents, even when she was pregnant). Bill began the systematic abuse of Sebastian when the boy was ten years of age, and when Duckett eventually left Addison's to set up his business, the workshop was located at 10 Canal Street.

In concluding her antipathy to the number, she wrote, *I don't even vote in general elections because I know that the winner will live at Number Ten.*

I was appalled, not only at her maltreatment but also at my superficial dislike of her. If I'd known even ten percent of this (there was that number ten yet again) I could have excused her arrogance and determination never to be beaten into submission. She had been beaten into such a state too many times by Duckett.

Searching forward through the document yet again, I learned that upon deciding to become an author, she vowed that the first victim in all her novels would meet a gruesome end on page ten.

I was satisfied. The issue was explained. It did not make for comfortable reading, but I could understand it in a perverse sort of way. We humans are plagued with superstition, and to Janet, it must have seemed that anything to do with a number ten had an almost satanic effect upon her life. By manipulating it into her novels, she probably felt that she was countering the hex. Whatever the twisted thought processes behind it, I could not doubt her success. By ensuring that the victims made their exit on page ten, she had made a fortune.

The underlying basis of her fortune, however, lay in Bill Duckett's death and the insurances which paid out. Before that he had kept her short of money. In discussing his demise, Anita maintained that she was initially suspicious. Like me, like Tony Wharrier, like Dennis, she was under the impression that her husband would never forget to set the locks on the auto lift, and her suspicions zoomed in on her son. From the age of ten, Sebastian was subject to his father's infrequent but persistent sexual abuse, which only stopped when he went off to Newcastle

University at the age of eighteen. The only time Anita saw her son during the next two years was when she drove up there. He would not come home, and when she eventually pushed him on the reason for his refusal, he told her what had been going on.

She confronted Bill, there was another argument, and it ended in the traditional manner when he beat her about the head. She spoke to Sebastian on the phone, he came home the following day, and when he saw what Bill had done to his mother, he blazed with anger.

Two years away had seen dramatic changes come over Sebastian. The little boy under the total control of his father, was gone. In his place was a fitness fanatic, a young man's body packed with muscle. He borrowed his mother's car, drove down to Canal Street, there was a confrontation, and Bill lashed out only to discover that his son was fitter, tougher, better able to look after himself. He beat his father and left him unconscious on the workshop floor.

Nathan's theory on the dog's silence was proven. The reason Sabre did not bark was because he knew both Bill and Sebastian.

After Bill was found dead, Anita brought up her suspicions and questioned Sebastian long before the police got to them, but he insisted that his father was alive when he left Canal Street. If Bill's death was anything but an accident, then it was someone other than her son. They never mentioned Sebastian's fight with Bill to the police, and when Paddy Quinn turned up no further evidence, Anita was satisfied that Bill had been left so dazed and confused by his son's attack, that he really did forget to set the locks on the auto lift. His death was, after all, an accident, due to negligence on Bill's part.

Her suspicions, however, gave her the idea for the first book, *Crushed*, a three hundred-page largely biographical novel, which in the space of a few months, notwithstanding the lack of professional editing, became a bestseller, and from there, Anita Stocker had it made. She persuaded Sebastian not to return to university, but to stay with her, acting as her security, for which he was paid a generous salary and 'company' car.

I felt that last phrase irritating. Dennis had had his own business for almost two decades, and I was not listed as an officer of the company, but I did the books for Haxford Fixers – well, Dennis's share of them anyway. I didn't get a salary, and I certainly didn't get a company car, although, to be fair, Dennis never charged me when he serviced or repaired my Renault. Even so, he put the spares, fluids, and other necessities through the books as 'sundry items'.

I was so engrossed in Anita's first draft autobiography that I barely notice the passage of time, and when I next looked at the clock, it was gone ten. Dennis was dozing in his wheelchair, Cappy the Cat was spark out in his basket and the television was playing to itself. My tea had long gone cold and the only reason I broke off was because I was in desperate need of the toilet. Strange, when you think that I'd not actually drunk the tea.

I nipped to the smallest room, came back via the kitchen where I switched on the kettle, and I gave Dennis a nudge. I asked if he needed to go to bed, he shook his head, and concentrated on the television again while I made fresh tea.

And while I waited for the kettle to boil, fussed over Dennis to make sure he was all right, let Cappy the Cat out, and stood savouring the cool evening in the open doorway, I thought about the things I had learned so far. I'd only made it as far as the release of *Crushed* and it remained to be seen whether Anita began to put together the real-life murders mirroring her fictitious episodes. She was an assiduous researcher, according to Val Wharrier, and for anyone determined to produce what she considered accurate if stomach churning fiction, it seemed unlikely that she had never made the connection before the police pulled her in for questioning a couple of days ago. If she knew, and without having any confirmation I was already certain of it, she must have had an idea who was responsible. And yet, she dismissed Sebastian as a suspect in Bill's death. There had to be someone else, someone in the background, perhaps even the hacker that Eddie Myner had conceivably uncovered.

I had vague recollections of Dennis going to bed sometime around half past eleven, but I sat at the laptop reading the unpublished biography, and sometime around midnight, I found what I was looking for. Not only found it, but it was as big a shock to me as it was to Anita.

From about three years after her initial success,

she knew of the similarity between real-life murders and her books, and yet the police, although they may well have been aware of it, never questioned her. If they had, she couldn't have told them anything. As a result, it took some time to realise that the first of these murders took place close to the release date of the relevant volume, and right away, she knew it was her son. Notwithstanding his denials, she had caught him reading her works in progress, and she realised he was materialising her fiction in real life.

She also knew what she should have done, but she did not.

I don't know when it happened, but something occurred to turn him from a self-assured twenty-year-old into a psychopath. Perhaps it was the way he beat his father in a straight fist fight, and the manner in which Bill died afterwards which gave him the taste for violence, and having developed that palate, working on the principle underlying my novel Crushed, he decided to take matters further.

Sebastian, I came to realise, was mentally unstable, a dangerous young man, but he was my son, and I loved him. How does a mother betray her son and commit him to lifelong incarceration? For that would be the outcome. I would lose him forever to the prison authorities or some asylum for the criminally insane.

I had the answer, perhaps not to the death of Bill Duckett, but certainly the murders of Fay Selkirk, Yolande Kalinsky, and how many others? Despite his denials on the morning I first met him, Sebastian did read his mother's raw manuscripts, and he committed the murders in keeping with her planned novels.

A glance at the clock told me it was coming up to one in the morning. It was far too late to ring Mandy or Paddy Quinn, and I couldn't ring Nathan because even now I didn't have his number.

I carried on reading, and I learned that after Yolande's murder, Anita confronted her son, told him that she knew, and a long argument followed. Afterwards, she became afraid that Sebastian would murder her in order to silence her, but she forestalled that.

When I gave my books their titles, I prepared some of those as a tribute to my son. The initial letters spell out his name. Not in the correct order, and they are not consecutive, but they spell Seb Duckett. When I realised he was a murderer, it also occurred to me that I might be on his list of victims, especially after I confronted him, so I set up another list of letters, which spell out the clear message, Sebastian Duckett is a psychopathic killer. The file is hidden on this computer, and it would take someone with a great deal of patience and no little expertise with words to not only find it but also crack the confusion of letters. Sebastian is aware of it, and that is my insurance against the danger of him turning on me.

When I read that paragraph, my fanciful notion of an anagram taken from the first letter of Nathan's ten listed books, became a reality. I took out the sheet of paper again, studied it, and wrote out the letters. CBDESTTKEU, and then began to strike them out in order, writing them in underneath, until

I had SEB DUCKETT.

From there, I made another search of a hard drive, seeking the file which she insisted contained a more informative message. I eventually found the file named 'keys' in a folder named 'admin', and the first line of the document was a long string of letters.

CYHBRLDSPEPSLITCIAHHSTKTOASTAKE ICNIAEU.

Once again I wrote the letters out, and began to strike them through, spelling out the message Anita insisted was there, until I had, SEBASTIAN DUCKETT IS A PSYCHOPATHIC KILLER.

Beneath it were pages and pages of different accounts of the various murders, and how Sebastian's whereabouts remained uncorroborated for a forty-eight hour period either side of those killings.

I knew that from a police point of view, these documents were no better than circumstantial evidence. Sebastian was not on any DNA database, had never been in trouble, and his fingerprints were not on file, but with this information, Paddy would have sufficient grounds to bring him in for questioning, those tests would be made, the prints and DNA compared to the results taken from Fay Selkirk's body, and even if they could not be linked to any of the earlier killings, he would still go to prison for life.

The only thing we were missing was Sebastian Duckett in person, and with the fear that another young man or woman was about to become a victim, I rang Mandy.

"Chrissy, do you know what time it is?"

"Yes, and I'm sorry, Mandy, but I have the evidence you need. Get Sebastian Duckett. He murdered Fay Selkirk, and at least nine other people. He's out of his tree, Mandy, and you have to get him off the streets as a matter of public safety."

"And you say you have evidence?"

"Yes. It's not definitive, but your forensic folk will take care of that."

"There's only one problem with this theory, Chrissy. As I told you earlier, he didn't murder his mother."

I'd forgotten about Anita's death. Having learned of her curious, but effective insurance policy, and made certain that Sebastian knew about it, he wouldn't have dared lay a finger on her.

"Right," I said. "I can't comment on that, Mandy, but he is responsible for the other killings. We can talk about his mother sometime tomorrow."

She must have looked at her watch. "You mean today."

Chapter Nineteen

I thought the house had turned into a telephone exchange when I woke at just after eight in the morning having had less than six hours sleep. The landline and the mobile never seemed to stop ringing.

First it was Dennis's alert and when I got to his room, he wanted the commode dealing with, but he'd waited so long, he'd already dealt with the problem and left me a mess to clear up in the bathroom. I know I shouldn't have been so irritable but frustration and a lack of sleep left me a little short with him, and he snapped back, "Juss tryin' telp."

I left him with breakfast and then disappeared into the bathroom to clean up the toilet and the floor. I was still at it when Nathan rang telling me he'd prepared the report for WDIG, his attempt to recover some money from them, and would I mind looking over it before he sent it off. "Written English isn't my strong suit."

"I'm tied up with all sorts this morning, Nathan. Could you email it to me, and I'll get back to you later?"

"No problem."

I gave him my email address, finished cleaning

up Dennis's mess, and then washed and dressed. No sooner had I pulled my shorty shorts into place than the phone rang again. It was Mandy this time. They had found Sebastian.

"And he's not a pretty sight. Been dead for hours."

My heart sank. "You'll need my evidence?"

"If you can manage to get it to us, yes."

"I'll come into the station... Oh, where did you find him?"

"His father's old workshop on Canal Street. Been empty since Bill Duckett clocked off and as you know, the council have the street scheduled for demolition when they can afford it."

I joined Dennis in the kitchen and was settling down for my breakfast, telling him I had to go to the police station, when Naomi rang and told me that both she and Bethany had been up and vomiting for most of the night. She blamed the pizza but I was all right. When Hazel McQuarrie told me she was feeling a bit off it, too, I worked out that it was probably the madeira cake I gave everyone at teatime. I was the only person who didn't have any, and it helped explain the mess Dennis had left me in the bathroom.

In Mrs McQuarrie's case, however, she had one of those cast-iron stomachs so prevalent in the generation before ours, and she agreed to sit in with Dennis while I went to the police station.

"About eleven o'clock," I told her.

I didn't feel like it. Tired, already feeling down thanks to a lack of sleep, the news of Sebastian's murder only made me feel worse, and before ever I spoke to Mandy, before I got ready and left the house, I knew that it was murder. His mother considered him mentally unstable, and considering the crimes he had committed, I would have to agree, but he was also a narcissist, obsessed with his own appearance, checking every reflective surface to ensure that he looked nothing less than perfection. 'He's not a pretty sight,' Mandy had said. Even if he was so far gone that he had decided to end it all, he would have done so cleanly, overdosing on drugs or painkillers or something, anything to ensure that even in death, he looked like his idea of an Adonis.

Hazel appeared at a couple of minutes to eleven, I gave her a quick résumé on Dennis's situation and what had happened in the bathroom, she promised to make him behave, and I left the house, climbing behind the wheel of our Fiat Diablo, inserted the key, and switched on the ignition, and at that moment, my Samsung smartphone tweeted to let me know an email had come in.

I started the engine, and sat for a moment or two, checking on it. Nathan. Short and sweet. *Report attached. Await your appro. Love. N.*

Love? Most people signed off with 'best', 'see ya', 'cheers' or something like that. Did this man still have the hots for me? As much as it did my ego good, it was an irrelevant question. With the need to get on, I closed down the email – I could look at the report later – backed out of the drive, and set off for the station.

One of my worst liabilities was my failure to take notes. I was notorious for it. But I hadn't made that mistake overnight. Before going to bed, I had noted particular passages in the manuscript, and then copied the job lot onto a memory stick, and when I sat with a pale, drawn and tired Mandy, and moody Paddy, I handed it over. While we enjoyed a cup of tea in comparative silence, they read through the pieces I had highlighted.

When they were both through with the reading, Paddy gave me a disapproving look. "I'm not arguing with the quality of the evidence, Chrissy, but it was procured illegally. You shouldn't have been copying files from her laptop."

"With the best will in the world, Paddy, it wasn't me. It was Nathan Evanson, Kalinsky whatever he wants to call himself. I just asked for a copy of the files. Besides, what difference does it make to you? You must have Anita's laptop, which means you have the originals."

Mandy yawned. "I'll check. The minute we're through talking to you. You obviously believe all of this, don't you?"

I stared at her bump. "You're not a parent yet, Mandy, so you might not be able to take it all in, but yes. I think Anita was telling the truth. You know, no matter what they do, what they've done, what they're likely to do, you never stop loving your children. That's probably not true of Bill Duckett, but it is for most of us. If it was Simon, I'd have handed him in the moment I realised, and he'd have been locked away for life, but that wouldn't stop me loving him. And now that he's dead, you won't have a problem getting Sebastian's DNA, and comparing it to Fay Selkirk's body, will you?"

"Already done," Paddy said. "It was him. We're

sure of it. There were plenty of traces of him on and around her body to tell us that he was with her. He even had her before he killed her. I think that just about wraps it all up, and it's not often you'll hear me say this, Chrissy, but we are grateful to you for your assistance."

Gratitude like that was unheard of coming from Paddy, and I accepted it gracefully. He'd been much kinder to me since The Incident. "Thank you, Paddy, but you still have the murder of Anita Stocker, Janet Duckett, call her what you will, outstanding, don't you?"

"We do."

"And you're not going to tell me what it is apart from the bruising to her body that convinces you there was someone else present."

He gave me an evil smile. That was more like the Paddy Quinn we all knew and not-so-secretly loathed. "Not this side of the next millennium."

While I was there, Mandy ran a check on Anita's laptop and found the same files I had read, whereupon she returned my memory stick and instructed me to make sure it was cleaned off once I got home. I agreed, with absolutely no intention of following the order, and came out into the hot sunshine yet again.

As I climbed into the car, I switched off flight mode on my phone, and right away, it tweeted to let me know there was another email. Nathan. Again. *Have you read the report yet. Love. N.*

I tutted to myself, and replied, *Just about to. C.*

I opened the report which was in PDF format, and it began with a long, rambling introduction to himself and me. As I read, fatigue began to overtake me, and I found myself distracted by thoughts of Anita Stocker. It was all very well to sit in judgement, insisting she was responsible for the complications and tragedy in her life, but was it accurate? Married to an abusive, violent husband, giving birth to a son who would eventually become a psychopath, would I have done things differently?

And to die like that… It did not bear thinking about, but thinking about it was exactly what I did. Paddy and Mandy were certain that someone else had been in that house, and it was a safe bet that it was someone related to one of Sebastian's victims. I discounted Nathan. He was with me on the day she died. So who, amongst the families and acquaintances of the other victims could be in the Haxford area?

The truth was, of course, it could be any of them. When you think of the UK, Haxford was not a million miles from anywhere. Cornwall, the furthest point in the south the country, was an eight-hour drive. The northern coast of Scotland, the furthest point in the opposite direction, was no more than nine or ten hours away by car. Wales was close enough, and as for Ireland, it only involved hopping on a ferry.

I didn't have the names of the real victims. Nathan had those. I was about to ring him, when I realised that a) he had called me from his room's phone and I still didn't have his mobile number, and b) my phone had gone to sleep again. I brought it to life, his PDF report stared out at me, so I concentrated on that instead. He was sure to ask when I got in touch with him.

I read again through the wordy introduction, and then moved on to the main thrust of his arguments.

Had Mrs Capper and I been able to demonstrate the truth of William Duckett's death, we would of contacted your good selves immediately, and you could have…

There's this thing that you often read in thrillers where the 'blood runs cold'. I don't know whether that's what happened to me, but it certainly felt like it. In that instant, all the pieces slotted together, and I knew what had happened at Hilly Farm on Friday morning. I climbed out of the car went into the police station, and after some earache from Vic Hillman, I got to speak to Mandy, she listened – she always did – and called on Paddy. He listened too, but had his doubts.

"You can pull him in on suspicion, Paddy," I said, "and while you have him, you could take prints, DNA, whatever you need."

"You're right, but it's very thin. Based on a spelling error?"

"Grammatical error, actually. And not the kind of error Anita Stocker would make. It's him, Paddy. Trust me."

From there, I was asked to wait, and ten minutes later, I settled into the rear seat of a patrol car alongside Mandy, and a small convoy left the station making for the Haxford Arms.

When we got there, a brief question to the manager confirmed that our quarry was still in his room, and with Paddy's permission, Mandy and I went up there and knocked on the door.

He greeted us with a smile. "Two gorgeous ladies." He eyed Mandy's bump. "One of them already satisfied. What can I do for you?"

I didn't smile. "I know it all, Nathan. I know exactly what you did on Friday morning, and I'm sure that by the time Paddy and Mandy are finished today, they'll know what you did to Sebastian last night."

He remained impassive. "You're being mysterious, Chrissy. What are you talking about?"

"You murdered Anita, and then you probably read parts of her autobiography, realised you got it wrong, saw that it was Sebastian, and you went out looking for him last night, found him, and murdered him too."

He laughed. "I was with you yesterday morning, remember? And as for Sebastian Stocker, I'm a stranger in Haxford. How would I know where to find him?"

"You were late getting to me, and Sebastian was well-known in this town. It wouldn't take much effort."

Mandy spoke up. "Whatever you have to say, you're going to have to say it formally. Nathan Kalinsky, I'm arresting you on suspicion of murder, I must caution you…"

Chapter Twenty

When we got back to the police station Nathan was taken to an interview room, where his fingerprints were taken, and a mouth swab for DNA analysis. He was advised of his right to legal representation, but declined, and was then left under guard while Paddy and Mandy made their preparations, the first of which was to put me in another interview room where they took another statement from me, but this time they concentrated on the sequence of events during Friday morning when Nathan arrived late at my place, and later when we got to Hilly Farm and discovered Anita's body. They were particularly interested in Nathan's act of collecting the washing-up gloves from the kitchen, and his use of the memory stick to copy Anita's files.

"He didn't use the keyboard at all?" Paddy asked.

"No. He touched only the mouse pad and control buttons."

I had an idea where they were going with this line of questioning, but I made no comment on it. From there, they asked more questions concerning our activities between the time I rang Mandy and the police arriving.

"We were sat on the settee. Mandy specifically

told us not to leave, not to go anywhere else in the house, and not to touch anything, which is exactly what we did."

"You didn't see him type out the brief suicide note?"

"No. That was already on the screen when we got there."

Paddy was satisfied and held up my statement. "We'll get this typed up, Chrissy, and ask you to sign it. In the meantime, I'm gonna break every rule in the book. We're going to question Kalinsky, and I'm gonna sit you in the observation room. Mandy will have an earpiece in. If he tries to mislead us, just give us the tip off. But, and this is important and you should already know it, you can't take any active part in the interview. All right?"

I nodded, and five minutes later, they installed me in the darkened observation room with a cup of tea at my elbow, and I watched through the two-way glass as they took their seats opposite Nathan and ran into the interview process, reminding him of his rights, offering to bring a solicitor, which he once again refused. Paddy left it to Mandy to spell out the seriousness of the situation, their suspicions, and she stressed that they had evidence from the crime scene which had yielded DNA samples, which in turn would be compared to his.

There's a misconception that DNA analysis takes days. A detailed analysis does indeed take many days, sometimes weeks, but mouth swabs can be analysed in a matter of hours, and the results are sufficient to establish identity and therefore bring charges.

Nathan took the information in his stride. "I don't deny that I was at Hilly Farm yesterday. Good heavens, woman, I was there with Christine Capper. She called you from Anita Stocker's front room."

"You were there earlier in the day murdering Anita," Mandy insisted. "It might interest you to know, Mr Kalinsky, that we found skin scales on the inside of a pair of washing-up gloves, and it's only a matter of waiting for the DNA analysis to establish that those skin scales are yours."

Nathan looked as cool and comfortable as I'd ever seen him, and I knew exactly what he was going to say. He put on this bashful sort of face, and said, "I do have a confession to make, but you're probably already aware of it. While we were waiting for you to arrive, I borrowed those washing-up gloves, and copied Anita's document files onto a memory stick. Either she or someone close to her murdered my daughter in Spain last year, and I had an idea that those documents might give me a lead. I know I shouldn't have done it, I hold my hand up, I admit it, and I'll handle whatever punishment is coming my way because of it. Be that as it may, it's obvious that you would find traces of me in those washing-up gloves. And as for the bruises to her wrist, I had hold of her wrists the day before when she attacked me. I was restraining her."

Paddy took over the challenge. "It might interest you to know, Kalinsky, that the bruises we found on her wrists do have your dabs, but those on her neck were made by someone wearing the washing-up gloves. When our people dusted the keyboard of that laptop, we found prints from those same washing-up gloves on a number of keys. When you found the computer, there was a single line of type on the screen." Paddy consulted his notes. "I quote, 'This can't go on. It has to end here. I should of done it sooner'. The keys on which we found those traces match exactly that sentence."

Nathan smiled. "Sentences."

"Again?"

"Sentences. Plural. Written English might not be my strong point, but there was more than one sentence."

From where I was sitting, I couldn't see Paddy's face, but I didn't need to. His words and tone were enough to tell me he was beginning to lose his temper. "As it happens, mister smarty-pants private eye, we have a detailed statement from Christine Capper, and she told us that when you and she visited, you did use the washing-up gloves to copy those files, but you made a point of not touching the keyboard. In fact, you typed that sentence earlier, and you used the washing-up gloves to try and hide your dabs. And the whole purpose was to make us believe that Anita had taken her own life."

Nathan shook his head. "And when am I supposed to have done this? I was with Christine Capper at her home yesterday morning. I didn't go anywhere near Hilly Farm until she was with me."

Now Mandy went on the attack. "Not so. DI Quinn just told you we have a detailed statement from Mrs Capper. She was expecting you at half past eleven yesterday morning, but you didn't get to her place until quarter to twelve. You told her you were here, at the police station, arguing the toss with Mr Quinn, but we know for a fact you weren't here. As we speak, some of our people are talking to staff at the Haxford Arms, and we already know that you weren't there either. Just get off your high horse, Kalinsky, and admit it. We know exactly where you were, we know what you were doing. Admit it, give us a full statement, you'll be charged, you will appear in court, but I'm sure the judge and jury will take into account the brutal murder of your daughter."

What came next took me slightly by surprise. Nathan lounged idly in his chair, and stared around the small room. For one moment, his eyes rested on the two-way glass between us, and it was almost as if he could see me. And then, without preamble, he admitted it.

"All right. You want the full story, I'll give you it. You've got most of it anyway, it's only a matter of time before you fill in the gaps. Yes, I went out to see her yesterday morning. I knew it was her. Right from the death of Bill Duckett, I knew she'd been murdering people and I figured it out as some bizarre means of lending an air of reality to the descriptions in her books. Twisted. Insane. But I wasn't in the same position as you're in with me right now. I had plenty of evidence, sure – the exact matches between the killings in her books and the real-life events – but I had no proof, and to be fair to myself, I really thought it was her. Well, you people should know what she was like. Arrogant, vain, completely self-centred. Thought she owned the world. When I challenged her, she started spitting, ranting, raving. She used the kind of language I haven't really heard since I came out of the army. Told me to eff off several times, so in the end, I got sick of waiting for her to own up. I went to the kitchen, took the washing-up gloves, picked up the knife, and told her she'd either confess, or she would find herself faced with my daughter the other side of the great curtain. She said, 'you don't have the guts'. So I grabbed hold of her, forced her into her chair, then grabbed the back of her neck and pushed her head forward so she could watch the blade slide into her chest, just below the breastbone, low enough to let her bleed to death. Obviously, she struggled. She tried to stop me. She even took hold of my wrist, but no way did she have that kind of strength. Then I stood back and watched her die like she'd watched my daughter die. Slowly and in a lot of pain. When I was happy that she was gone, I removed all traces of me from the knife, and clamped her hands around the handle in such a manner that her prints would be on it and everyone would believe she'd taken her own life in a fit of remorse. Then, still wearing the washing-up gloves, I opened up the laptop, and typed that little message. Once I was through, I jumped in the car and drove down to Christine's place." He shook his head sadly. "I was hyped up, not thinking straight. If I had been, I'd have dumped the washing-up gloves, I'd have taken a copy of the document files there and then, but none of that occurred to me. I was late for my appointment with Christine, and that was at the forefront of my mind."

Mandy was writing furiously, trying to keep up with the voluble flow of words coming from him.

Meanwhile Paddy carried on applying the pressure.

"It wasn't her. It was her son, Sebastian."

"Yes, I didn't get to the real truth until last night in my hotel room and I found draft chapters from her proposed autobiography. I told you. At the time I went to Hilly Farm, I really thought it was her." His face took on a look of almost pleading, the first sign of any weakness I'd seen him display since we met. "I didn't go there with the intention of killing her. She should have confessed. Obviously, I didn't realise that she was protecting her son, but even so, if she'd told me that he was the man we'd all been seeking I'd have collared the pair of them and handed them over to you. She'd have still been alive. And so would he."

When Paddy next spoke, there was a hint of satisfaction about his voice. "Let's turn our attention to Sebastian. We found him in the derelict industrial units on Canal Street. The unit his father used to own. He'd been beaten to death. Traces of God knows how many people there, and when we get down to it, I'm sure we'll find traces of you. There's no point in denying it. You killed him. Tell us what happened."

Nathan let out a long sigh. "When I got back to my hotel last night, I was looking through Anita's documents, as I've already said, I found the draft of her autobiography. When I read it, I was appalled. I'd killed the woman and she was innocent. All she had ever done was protect her son, and I could understand that. He butchered my daughter, put her through hell, stood and watched her bleed to death. If I could have protected my daughter the same way

Anita protected him, I would have done. So, about nine o'clock last night, I went out looking for him. I found him in some club called Jumping Jacks. He gave me some lip, but I managed to get him outside, and I confronted him with the truth. He denied it, obviously, but then I told him I'd read his mother's autobiography, and I knew everything, and I'd already murdered her instead of him. He lost it. Went for me." Nathan laughed. "As if. A poser. That's what he was. I flattened him, threw him into my car, went through his pockets, found the keys to Canal Street. That idiot, even had the key labelled. So I took him down there, got him inside, and told him that unless he was ready to admit everything to you people, I would batter him to death. He was up for the fight, so I gave him a fight. He lost. And if you expect me to say I'm sorry about that, you've got a long wait ahead of you. He was an animal. I don't care about the abuse he suffered under his father. He was a sadistic psychopath, a mad dog, and we all know that the best way to deal with mad dogs is to put them down. So I put him down." He shrugged. "And there you have it. I killed her, I killed him."

I was satisfied, but the police weren't. Not yet.

"One last point," Mandy said. "Eddie Myner."

Nathan chuckled. "He's lucky to be alive. I actually hit him on Thursday evening. He sent Christine a text telling her that he'd managed to hack into Anita's system. It was a bad idea of Christine's because he was sure to learn of at least one other hack … mine. How do you think I knew about *Utter Carnage*? How do you think I knew to tip you people off over the phone? There was a bit of a debate. He'd had fifty off Christine so I offered him another hundred to shut up, and he wouldn't play ball. When he agreed to take a job on, he did the job, end of story. Things got a bit heated, he went for me, so I knocked the hell out of him, left him unconscious on the floor and trashed his gear." Nathan shook his head sadly. "Will these geeks never learn not to take on real men?" He raised his eyebrows at the police. "Will he live?"

"He won't be hacking other people's computers for a while," Paddy said, "but he should be fit to give evidence by the time you come to trial." Paddy stood up. "Sergeant Hiscoe, charge him."

Chapter Twenty-One

The police might have finished with him, but there were still one or two outstanding issues between Nathan and me, and as Paddy came out of the interview room, I emerged from the observation room and collared him.

"Is there any chance I could have two minutes with him?"

"Not this side of hell freezing over. You know the score, Christine."

"Come on, Paddy. You know me better than that, and I'm not looking to let him off the hook. There are things between me and him I need to sort out for my own peace of mind. I'm not going to give him an alibi or anything like that, I just need the answers to one or two questions, personal questions."

He looked down his nose at me in a manner which he hadn't done since before The Incident. "He's had your trolleys off?"

I struggled to control a flash of temper. "No he has not. Please, Paddy. I was grateful to you for the way you helped after what happened to Dennis, and I know it's unusual, but I'm asking you this one favour."

The tiny hint of my gratitude swung the exchange in my favour. "You get five minutes, and

I'll have a uniform sit in."

There was a delay before Mandy emerged from the interview room carrying her statement and the CD upon which the interview had been recorded. Paddy explained the situation, and I was allowed in, accompanied by Rehana Suleman. As we went in, I said to Rehana, "You might have to close your ears at some of this, love. It's personal."

She smiled. "Diplomatically deaf when I need to be, Chrissy."

I sat down facing Nathan. He studied me with a faint, good-humoured smile, as though he were taking a rise out of me. I was about to go into my semi-rehearsed diatribe, when he beat me to it.

"How did you know it was me?"

"Two things, and Paddy and Mandy have already covered one angle. Yesterday morning, you told me you were with Paddy at the police station, which is why you were late getting to my place. And yet, when we were out at Hilly Farm, Paddy insisted that he'd told you two days prior to that about Bill Duckett. I didn't twig it at first, but when I did, I knew you weren't at your hotel and you weren't at the police station. It was only later that it occurred to me that you were at Hilly Farm, probably pressuring Anita, and when she wouldn't admit to killing your daughter, you killed her instead."

"Chrissy—"

"I said there were two things. The other is your standard of written English. You even admitted it when you asked me to look over the report. Well, I did, and everything became crystal clear. I quote, 'Had Mrs Capper and I been able to demonstrate the truth of William Duckett's death, we would of contacted your good selves immediately'. Would of? It should be would *have*. And then I suddenly realised where I'd seen the same mistake before. It was Anita's short suicide note, that single line on her laptop screen. 'I should of done it sooner'. She was a novelist, a professional writer. You might not like her work, but you couldn't fault her standard of English. There is no way she would have written 'of' instead of 'have'. That was one of the things that told me she didn't commit suicide. And the same applied to Sebastian. He was well educated. University, even though he never graduated. You're not. You were a square basher, an NCO when you came out of the army. A loud voice is compulsory, a good education, necessary, and I assume a top class standard of written English might be useful but not it's vital. Your report for the police and the insurance company sealed the deal."

He gave me a small, mock round of applause. "Well done. You know you're a good detective, Chrissy. Much better than you make yourself out to be. When I first came to your place looking for Dennis, I had you down as a bog standard, Haxford housewife, a head full of gossip, housework, shopping for groceries, wondering when the old man would next want a bit of the other, and surfing the shopping channels. I was wrong. I underestimated you."

"You're not the first and I dare say you won't be the last." I felt like my fury would explode any second now. "Two days ago, you almost had me laid under you. What was that all about? What if you'd got your way? Would you have dispatched me the way you did Anita?"

He chuckled. "You're taking this all too personally. I told you about Thursday, although I have to admit, I wasn't entirely truthful, so don't flatter yourself. I've met your kind of middle-aged woman before. All prim and prissy on the surface, but secretly waiting for me to whip their knickers off and give them a good time. You're a classic case. Not a bad looking woman, but hardly a centrefold, and with your husband the way he is, I figured you might be getting desperate for it, so I chanced my arm. You said no, and that was an end of it. No way would I ever force you. And murder you? Never. Sebastian Duckett did that to my daughter, and there is no way I would ever inflict that kind of pain on any woman... Anita Stocker excepted." Now he laughed. "Chalk it down to experience, Chrissy, and go back to looking after Dennis. It's what you were born to do."

I stood up, ready to leave. "For all his failings, for all his temporary disability, I'd rather have Dennis than ten men like you. I'm sorry for what happened to your daughter, but that didn't give you the right to play God, and as for me... the only thing I'm desperate for is getting away from you." I turned and marched out of the interview room.

I left the police station, climbed into my car, and started the engine. I was shaking with anger coming from several sources. His matter-of-fact manner in the face of his crimes, almost as if he felt he had the right to murder both Anita and Sebastian, and beat Eddie Myner to a pulp.

But the greater part of my irritation came from his attitude to me, and by default to middle-aged women in general. What was it he said? Prim and prissy on the surface, but secretly waiting for him to slide their undies off and give them a good time. His assumption that I was getting desperate, compounded by his lies in the face of my challenge made my blood boil. We can all jump to the wrong conclusions about the people we meet, but the thought that I could actually be giving out such an impression infuriated me.

If I was in a bad mood when I left the police station, I didn't expect it to get worse when I got home, but when I walked through the house and stepped out into the back garden, I found Dennis… alone. Mrs McQuarrie was supposed to be with him, but there was no sign of her. Had she wheeled him out into the garden and then left him? It didn't seem likely. She was normally so reliable.

I hurried to him "How come you're out here? Has Hazel just left you here?"

He scowled up at me. "No." He looked away from me. "Teld her t'go. I gorrear m'self."

Over the last twenty-four hours, he had been steadily improving, but I'd already seen him guide that wheelchair down the steep ramps to the decking, but to take on the second slope down into the garden was, in my opinion, a risk too far. "That's dangerous, Dennis," I insisted. "What if you'd lost control?"

"Didn't."

When he was fully fit it was rare that I saw him in such a mood, and something was clearly amiss now. I didn't like to pressure him, but considering the torrid time I'd had of things over the last few days, the last thing we needed was sulks between the two of us. I had to get to the bottom of it.

"What's wrong, love?"

"Nowt."

It was time to get just a little tougher with him. "This is your wife you're talking to, Dennis. After thirty years, you can't hide anything from me. Now tell me what is wrong." He knew that tone of voice. One that demanded answers and would not go away until it had them.

He looked away again, staring round the garden, turning his head to look back at the house, and then eventually looked me in the eye.

It took time. Not that he was reluctant to say what was on his mind, but I had the problem of translating everything he said into normal English. What follows, is that translation.

When he finally faced me, he said, "I know about you and him. Golden boy. Your fancy man."

"You mean Nathan?"

"Who else? The other day, was it yesterday, I needed you to empty the chamber pot, I'd already got myself out of bed to use it. You even saw me manage all on my own later in the afternoon, when we were all round the patio table. So you knew I could manage for myself. Going back to yesterday morning, when I heard you talking to him in the kitchen, I thought I'd show you how good I was getting, and I did it. Got myself out of bed, into the wheelchair, and I was wheeling it along the hall when I heard you talking about how it was part of his plan to get your pants off out on the moors and give you a good seeing to so you'd agree to work with him. You even asked him if he knew you were hard up for it."

"Dennis—"

He didn't wait for me to explain. "It hurts, Chrissy. It flaming well hurts, but I understand."

A tear began to form in his eye and I remembered that after the debate between Nathan and I had calmed and I learned about his daughter, I made an excuse and left the kitchen to spend a few minutes alone. As I passed along the hall, I checked on Dennis. He'd been crying and I assumed it was self-pity, and I suppose it was in a way. But it had nothing to do with his injuries. He'd overheard my conversation with Nathan, and put the wrong, but understandable interpretation on it. His wife had been unfaithful to him.

"The sex thing," he went on. "It's not the be all and end all for you. I know that. But it's important, and I can understand you needing to deal with it. And another bloke is the only option you've got, and I'll have to deal with that. I can forgive you. Everything you've had to put up with this last month, it doesn't surprise me, and I'm not annoyed with you, but I can't pretend it doesn't hurt."

I kept my voice soft. "Dennis, what you heard was completely out of context."

"Chrissy—"

"No. Please listen to me, Dennis. You have to hear me out, because I promise you nothing happened between Nathan Kalinsky and me. He tried his luck. He kissed me, got his hands to my bottom, tried to get under my skirt but I stopped him. I promise you, it was no more than that. I couldn't do that to you. Not just with Nathan, but with any man."

"You don't need to explain, Chrissy."

"Oh but I do because you've got the wrong end of the stick." I gave him a naughty smile. "And I didn't get the end of any stick from him. Believe me, Dennis, he tried, I said no. What you heard was me demanding answers from him as to why he even bothered trying. It wasn't as if I'd done anything to encourage him. I never would do anything like that because aside from the fact that I'm not interested, I know how much it would hurt you."

"Honest?"

"Honest. I would never betray you, Dennis."

He appeared slightly surprised. "Why not? I just said I know how much you like it. And you're entitled. Anyone is. And what good am I to you?" His face fell and his mood dived again. "I'm not a man anymore. I can't work, I can't walk, I can't even think or talk properly half the time." Now his eyes burned into me. "And I can't do what a bloke's supposed to do for his wife when she wants. The ruddy cat's more use to you now. At least he keeps the mice away." He let out a frustrated sigh. "I'm just a blinking nuisance, a pain in the backside, a pill stone round your neck."

This was a side of him I hadn't seen much of over the last three decades. In his own way he was trying to tell me he loved me, but for a Haxforder, 'I love you,' is wussy, especially coming from a man. The last time I could truly recall him using those three forbidden words was when he turned up to see me on the maternity ward and looked down on his new daughter.

I held his hand. "You mean a millstone."

"Happen I do."

"Well, you're right. You are a millstone, you are pain in the bottom, you are a blinking nuisance, but you're my blinking nuisance, Dennis, and I would never do anything to hurt you. And you will get better. You've come on so much over the last twenty-four hours, and that means you're on the mend. It won't be long before you're ignoring everything but the fine tuning on a compact Kia or a Fiat."

"I hate Kias and I'm not fond of Fiats."

I laughed. "That's more like my Dennis." More seriously, I said, "As for the other… well, yes, it's important, but not to the point of destroying us."

"What about Mr wonderful? Has he gone back to Bradford?"

"York, actually, and no. He's on his way to jail for a long time. Forget him, love. If we ever see him again, it'll be too soon." I squeezed his hand, love flowing from me to him. "We're what's important, not him, and I'm looking forward to getting my husband back, fit, going back to work, moaning about modern cars and drooling over classics. And I know that one fine night you'll take me by surprise, whisk me off to bed and give me the time of my life."

He tried to smile. "And then I'll be Mr wonderful?"

"Dennis, you're already Mr wonderful for me."

Epilogue

Nathan's confession to the murders of Janet and Sebastian Duckett saw him brought to trial months later, and despite his plea of diminished responsibility in the aftermath of his daughter's horrific death, he was found guilty and sentenced to life imprisonment.

When I gave evidence, his defence accused me of being a vindictive, jilted lover, but I rejected both accusations, first denying that Nathan and I had ever been lovers, and then dismissing the barrister's further insistence that I only went to the police out of spite.

After the trial, Kim did ask me about it, and she said that in my position she would have a) probably let him have his way in the long grass and b) kept her mouth shut about his treatment of Anita, but I remained unrepentant. Rule of law does not permit vigilante justice, and besides, Anita had lived in love and in fear of Sebastian for many years, her safety only assured by the details locked away in her draft autobiography. If Nathan had controlled his fury for one more day, we would have had Sebastian and with him taken out of the equation, I was sure Anita would have told us everything.

I never did get paid. Anita was no longer with us

to be able to pay me, although I did have the option of claiming on her estate when it was finally sorted out. I'd torn up the contract with Val Wharrier. To be fair, she may have led me into the case, but beyond that she had nothing to do with it. I did get in touch with WDIG and they were not willing to negotiate. There was no guarantee that they would ever get back one penny of the amount they'd paid out on Bill Duckett's death.

All that said, I did pick up a hundred pounds from the Haxford Recorder when they interviewed me after Nathan was sentenced, and on the strength of my sudden, increased fame, Radio Haxford upped my weekly fee by ten pounds. It was a long way from providing Dennis and me with the level of financial security we had before The Incident, but as the old saying goes, every penny helps.

Something much more important than money came out of the case: personal validation. I substantiated and reinforced my belief in myself, my fidelity, my absolute faith in my marriage. I've never made any claim to my (theoretical) beauty or allure, but under extreme pressure when every fibre of my being tempted me to abandon everything, go for it, lie back and enjoy it, I fell back on my founding principles and rejected Nathan's Kalinsky's advances.

Perhaps more important was a reawakening of the way I saw Dennis. Always obsessed more with the mechanical than mating, I realised that deep down, I was more important to him than any motor car. Just as important as he was to me. Perhaps more so. He was willing to tolerate the pain of adultery to compensate for his temporary lack of ability. That level of sacrifice can only come from a man possessed of an ingrained understanding of his partner and her desires, and an acceptance of his physical inability to deal with them, and even though I would never consider such a course of action, I loved him all the more for it.

Dennis still had a mountain to climb before he was back to his old self, but I would climb it alongside him, and with the closure of the case, I faced the future with a little more optimism.

And on that note, I'll bid you good day. Tune in next week to Christine Capper's Comings & Goings, when I'll have more tales from Haxford and the surrounding area.

THE END

The Author

David W Robinson retired from the rat race after the other rats objected to his participation, and he now lives with his long-suffering wife in sight of the Pennine Moors outside Manchester.

Best known as the creator of the light-hearted **Sanford 3rd Age Club Mysteries**, and in the same vein, the brand new series, **Mrs Capper's Casebook**. He also produces darker, more psychological crime thrillers; the Feyer & Drake thrillers and occasional standalone titles.

He, produces his own videos, and can frequently be heard grumbling against the world on Facebook at **https://www.facebook.com/dwrobinson3** and has a YouTube channel at **https://www.youtube.com/user/Dwrob96/videos**. For more information you can track him down at **www.dwrob.com** and if you want to sign up to my newsletter and pick up a #FREE book or two, you can find all the details at **https://dwrob.com/readers-club/**

By the same author

(All titles are exclusive to Amazon)

Self-Published works
As David W Robinson
Mrs Capper's Christmas
Death at the Wool Fair
Blackmail at the Ballot Box
Exit Page Ten

Titles published and managed by Darkstroke Books

The Sanford 3rd Age Club Mysteries
The Filey Connection
The I-spy Murders
A Halloween Homicide
A Murder for Christmas
Murder at the Murder Mystery Weekend
My Deadly Valentine
The Chocolate Egg Murders
The Summer Wedding Murder
Costa del Murder
Christmas Crackers
Death in Distribution
A Killing in the Family
A Theatrical Murder
Trial by Fire
Peril in Palmanova
The Squires Lodge Murders
Murder at the Treasure Hunt
A Cornish Killing

Merry Murders Everyone
Tales from the Lazy Luncheonette Casebook
A Tangle in Tenerife
Tis the Season to Be Murdered
Confusion in Cleethorpes
Murder on the Movie Set
A Deadly Twixmas

The Midthorpe Mysteries
Missing on Midthorpe
Bloodshed in Benidorm

Feyer & Drake
The Anagramist
The Frame

Standalone titles
The Cutter
Kracht

THANK YOU FOR READING. I HOPE YOU
HAVE ENJOYED THIS BOOK. IF SO IT
WOULD BE WONDERFUL IF YOU COULD
LEAVE A REVIEW ON AMAZON?